What the critics are saying…

"Kiss of Heat is an exceptional journey of loss, love, and acceptance. Ms. Leigh does not disappoint with this the next chapter in the feline breed series. If you have been anxiously waiting for the next chapter in the breeds series then this book is a must read." ~Reviewed by Dianne Nogueras, eCataRomance Reviews

"Lora Leigh's signature of deep emotional relationships between her characters is again in the forefront. Her continuity from one book to the next is amazing as we garner greater knowledge into the worlds she builds." ~Reviewed by Gail, Romance Junkies

"I've enjoyed all the books in the Wolf Breeds and the Feline Breeds series so far, and I think this one is the best one of them all." ~Reviewed by S. Khaw, The Road to Romance

"The intense passion between the main characters is still there, as is the vividly erotic love scenes, action galore and the intriguing twists in the plot. There is subtle difference in this book, but I will leave it to you to discover that indefinable something. I will tell you this: beg, borrow, or steal the time away from your busy day to read this book! I promise you will not regret one stolen moment." ~Reviewed by Cynthia, A Romance Review

Tempting the Beast

This book received a JERR Gold Star Award

"The story grabs you by the collar and pulls you in, showing you the majesty of the mountains where the pride lives, the loyalty and commitment they have for each other, and that human nature can overcome tremendous obstacles and still survive. This book deserves all the accolades that it is garnering." ~*Reviewer: Oleta M. Blaylock, Just Erotic Romance Reviews*

The Man Within

Book 2 in the Feline Breeds series
This book received a JERR Gold Star Award

"The Man Within deserves a gold star because it really puts you in the mind of the breeds. ...This novel puts in motion the question of if another species did exist that is half human how would you react to them, acceptance or fear of the unknown? ...I believe that Lora Leigh has created a story that makes you review your stand on these issues, by getting into the minds of the breeds she shows us what it is like to be on the other side. All of these things combined make this an awesome novel for the Gold Star Award." ~*Reviewer: Angel Brewer, Just Erotic Romance Reviews*

Elizabeth's Wolf

ELIZABETH'S WOLF received a PERFECT TEN from: Romance Reviews Today

"Dynamic, humorous, passionate and stirring, ELIZABETH'S WOLF is erotic romance at its best. Don't miss it." ~*Reviewed by Sondrea Cash*

LORA LEIGH

KISS OF HEAT

FELINE BREEDS 3

ELLORA'S CAVE
ROMANTICA PUBLISHING

An Ellora's Cave Romantica Publication

www.ellorascave.com

Feline Breeds: Kiss of Heat

ISBN # 1419953400
ALL RIGHTS RESERVED.
Feline Breeds: Kiss of Heat Copyright© 2004 Lora Leigh
Edited by: Sue-Ellen Gower
Cover art by: Syneca

Electronic book Publication: May, 2004
Trade paperback Publication: November, 2005

Warning:

The following material contains graphic sexual content meant for mature readers. *Feline Breeds: Kiss of Heat* has been rated E-*rotic* by a minimum of three independent reviewers.

Ellora's Cave Publishing offers three levels of Romantica™ reading entertainment: S (S-ensuous), E (E-rotic), and X (X-treme).

S-*ensuous* love scenes are explicit and leave nothing to the imagination.

E-*rotic* love scenes are explicit, leave nothing to the imagination, and are high in volume per the overall word count. In addition, some E-rated titles might contain fantasy material that some readers find objectionable, such as bondage, submission, same sex encounters, forced seductions, etc. E-rated titles are the most graphic titles we carry; it is common, for instance, for an author to use words such as "fucking", "cock", "pussy", etc., within their work of literature.

X-*treme* titles differ from E-rated titles only in plot premise and storyline execution. Unlike E-rated titles, stories designated with the letter X tend to contain controversial subject matter not for the faint of heart.

Kiss of Heat

Feline Breeds

Dedication

For Sondrea and Terry. For hours of Internet tech support and for understanding just how computer dumb I could be. And as always, thank you for the friendship.

Trademarks Acknowledgement

The author acknowledges the trademarked status and trademark owners of the following wordmarks mentioned in this work of fiction:

Viagra: Pfizer Inc.

Garfield: Paws, Incorporated

Oreos: Nabisco Brands Company

Prologue
Sandy Hook

Sherra stood silently in the shadows of the motel, watching carefully, her eyes narrowed as the nine men parted company and went to their respective rooms. They were furious, but one was coldly dangerous. She had watched them at the airport after dropping Doc off at the safe house, then followed them to Sandy Hook and watched as they checked in.

Kane didn't remind her of Merinus in any way. He was darker-haired, the color nearly black, with intense, cold blue eyes. His strong jaw and high cheekbones gave a hint to Native American ancestry, his hard, graceful body hinting at extensive military training. She knew the look, the way a killer moved. She had grown up among them, been raped by them more than once. But this one she knew personally.

This man had brought her pleasure. Despite her pleas, despite her wishes to the contrary, he had taken her beneath the unfeeling eye of a camera, riding her from one climax to the next, his lust fueled by hers, and hers by his touch.

Had it only been eleven years ago? Sweet heaven, that night tormented her even now, as though it had happened only yesterday. The dark soldier who had sworn to help her, to rescue her. He had come to her, holding freedom in one hand, her heart in the other, and spent the night teaching her the pleasures of her woman's body. When he left, he never returned. But the doctors had. They had returned to her cell with the video they had taped of the night she spent with him. They had snickered at the things Kane Tyler had done to her, that she had done to him, all in the name of science. Rape had not impregnated her. They had wondered if pleasure would.

She was a Breed. As she had been taught in the Genetics Council's labs, she wasn't human, she was an animal in human form, nothing more. Even now, ten years after her freedom from those labs, she wasn't certain which she was. Human or animal. She knew, for a very brief time, in this man's arms, she had become a woman. And she would hate him for it until she drew her last breath.

She had been created, not born. Trained, not raised. When Kane touched her, she had lived. When he deceived her she had lost the only thing that ever mattered in her life, and now, life or death, it didn't matter. All that mattered was the survival of the Pride itself.

Their sanctuary here in Sandy Hook had been compromised in ways that could never be repaired now. They were, once again, homeless. Homeless and hunted.

Her hands clenched into fists of rage as Kane lingered outside his room, lazily finishing a cigarette he had lit moments earlier. She wanted to kill him now. She had sworn she would kill him if she ever found him again. Sworn she would see to it that he paid for every moment of pain she suffered all those years ago. She had sworn he would pay for lying to her, and for doing it so easily without her knowledge. He had betrayed her, just as he had betrayed his sister.

His expression hardened when the last door finally closed and he was left alone with her.

"Where's Merinus?" His voice was savage, pulsating with a fury that sent a frisson of unease through her body. How had he known she was there, watching him, waiting? "And why the fuck weren't we met at the airport as promised?"

"I have a better question," she said from the safety of the shadows. "Why would a brother betray a sister he swears to love, on the eve of promised help?"

He turned around slowly, casually, until he was facing her. She saw hard purpose in his face, and surprise.

"What the hell are you talking about?"

"A full team of soldiers swept over Callan's house. A dozen men. All I know for sure is that they didn't get him or Merinus. But I know they want her. They know about her."

"Know what, for God's sake?" He raked his fingers through his hair, his voice quiet but rough with fury. "Why the hell would they attack now?"

"They know your sister has mated with Callan," she told him carefully. "Just as you knew."

Or had he? She watched his face pale alarmingly, his blue eyes widening.

"That bastard touched her?" he snarled.

"No," she drawled mockingly. "He mated with her. Surely you remember the concept? And now the Council no longer cares if they take him alive or dead. They want the woman and any child she carries. But you already knew that, didn't you, Mr. Tyler? Why else would they attack mere hours after talking to you?"

He shook his head slowly.

"I never betrayed my sister. I wouldn't." His voice sent a chill down her spine.

Sherra frowned.

"I came to kill you, Kane Tyler," she said carefully.

He didn't seem surprised now. His mouth was edged with mockery.

"Perhaps you could delay that little attempt long enough for me to save my sister's ass," he growled. "What the hell is this mating shit?"

"Later," she snapped. "Now is not the time for explanations. Now is the time for you to tell me how the Council learned of the mating, if Merinus didn't tell you of it."

And Sherra was nearly certain he hadn't known. He was a liar, but in this one instance, he was telling the truth. Her gifts had grown through the years, with maturity and desperation. She could now smell a lie as others could diseased trash.

"Who are you?" His voice sizzled. "And you're going to have to be a little more forthcoming than you have been, woman. I can't help Merinus or Callan with so little information."

Taking a deep breath, Sherra stepped from the shadows. She watched his eyes widen, saw the suspicion turn to knowledge.

"You aren't dead," he whispered, blinking, as though trying to assure himself she was there. His expression went slack with shock, his eyes gleaming beneath the low lights with at first something resembling hope, then with fury.

Bitterness filled her with a wave of pain so intense, she nearly drowned beneath it. He was furious now, and he had no right to be.

"No, lover, I wasn't killed. But that doesn't mean you have much longer to live."

Sherra faced her past now as she never had before. Nightmares and broken hopes fragmented around her, drawing her soul into a bleak, dark void she feared she could never escape. She felt the surging lust, the need, just as Callan and Merinus knew it, thundering through her blood, through her very being. Before her stood the man who had betrayed her years before. In a bleak, cold lab, his body laboring over her, throwing her into pleasure despite every barrier she put up against it. Her mate. The father of the child she had lost. The one man she had sworn to kill.

She was alive. Kane stared at her, hiding the tremble in his hands, the need welling inside him like a dark, hungry cloud. How many years had he dreamed of her, needed her, longed for her with every fiber of his being? And now she was here, standing before him, shrouded in darkness, her eyes glittering with hatred.

Hatred.

He swallowed past the emotion clogging his throat, the regret lancing his chest and the disbelief he couldn't seem to shake. As though the world had shifted on its axis, pitching him into a world that was as different as it was the same the day before.

"Why didn't you contact me?" He could barely force the words past his lips. She was alive, had been all these years. He had suffered through hell, ached until he swore his soul was a raw, open wound, and all this time, she had been alive.

She sneered. A cold curve to her lips that twisted in his soul as he watched her. Fingers as slender and graceful as life itself reached beside her to pluck a delicate white blossom from the thick bush at her side. They tore at the petals, ripping them casually from their delicate mooring and leaving them to drift in wounded splendor to the ground.

Staring at her was tearing his soul to pieces. Realizing she had been alive, all this time, free, and she hadn't contacted him, hadn't even bothered to let him know, was destroying the last thread of sanity he thought he had held onto all these years.

"Goddamn you!" he snarled, fury surging inside him, so hot, so deep it blistered the open wounds her "death" had left years ago. "All these fucking years, and not even a goddamned phone call, Sherra? Nothing?"

He had to clench his fingers into fists to keep from jerking her to him, to hold back the lust and burning rage filling his mind. He was literally seeing red. The haze at the edge of his vision rippled and burned, turning the soft fall of the hotel lights into a bloody aura.

Her gaze flickered over him, cold, unemotional, filled with victorious triumph.

"And I would have done that why?" She bared her teeth, her hatred crisp, clear, lining the beauty of her expression with remorseless hatred.

He fell back a step, feeling the blow to the pit of his soul. He had bled for her. Had nearly died for her. For this. Her hatred.

"No reason." His voice was hoarse, and he hated her for that. Hated the emotion tearing his heart to pieces as she watched him with the glimmer of amusement in her eyes. "No reason at all."

Merinus was all that mattered now. His sister and the man who held her.

"Where's my sister?"

"She's safe." She shrugged again. "That's all you need to know."

He moved before she could blink. He had known his only edge would be whatever surprise he could gain. He took the advantage fiercely. His hands caught her wrists, twisting them quickly behind her back, holding them in a steel-hard grip as he pushed her roughly against the side of the motel.

"Wrong," he snarled. "That is not all I need to know, nor is it all you will tell me. By God, I nearly died for you and your fucking Pride once, but I'll be damned if Merinus will be hurt any further." His free hand gripped the long silken hair, his fingertips transmitting the sensation of cool, perfect pleasure to his brain even as he fought it. Her body pressed against him, still, unyielding as her eyes widened in shock.

"You're crazy," she snapped. "No more games, Kane, you betrayed us all…"

He wanted to shake her, wanted to howl in misery. "You believe what the hell you want to now, Sherra. I really don't give a fuck. But you will tell me what the hell is going on and you will do it now. Or so help me God I'll make you wish you had."

Hunger ambushed him. His cock swelled to painful, immediate erection, his mouth watered for the taste of her, the scent of her body made him sweat, made his balls draw up in lust. Eleven fucking years. Eleven years without her, craving her taste, her touch. For what? For fucking nothing.

"You will tell me." He pressed his cock into her lower belly, watched her pale, watched the fear that flickered in the shadows of her eyes as his heart twisted in misery. "Or I'll show you, *lover*, the bastard you believe I can be."

Only Merinus mattered. For now.

Chapter One
Five months later

"Afternoon, kitty." Kane's deliberate drawl as Sherra entered the kitchen, prepared for the weekly meeting Callan insisted on, had the hair on the back of her neck rising in instant defense. That drawl never indicated a pleasant conversation where Kane was involved.

It wasn't as if any conversation she had with him was ever pleasant. He insisted on provoking her at every opportunity and generally did his level best to see just how angry he could make her.

His blue eyes were cool, calculating, watching her with an amused mockery that made her ache to scratch them out. That need was in direct conflict with the overpowering urge to fuck him silly. She was in heat. She hated it but had no choice except to admit to it. After eleven long years of pain and fear, she now knew why her body turned traitor on her, beginning with an overwhelming arousal and ending with a bleak, almost agonizing pain before slowly diminishing. For one month of each year, she had been going into heat. And she had suffered because her mate had already taken her, had already programmed her body to accept no other touch but his.

If he had been a Breed, she could have understood it. Merinus and Roni had been marked by their mates, their bodies conditioned by the hormonal fluids that eased from the swollen glands just under the men's tongues. But Sherra knew that on the single night she had spent with Kane her own hormonal glands hadn't been active. And she sure as hell hadn't made the mistake of kissing him since he had barged back into her life. Not since learning the signs of the mating heat and knowing beyond a shadow of a doubt that Kane was her mate.

He was leaning negligently against the kitchen counter, cup in hand, his tall, leanly muscled body relaxed and tempting. His jeans bulged between his thighs. She swallowed, dragging her gaze away from him. He was hard and ready to fuck. And only God knew just how badly she wanted him to come into her. Strong and thick, his cock surging up her wet pussy until she screamed. She almost shivered at the thought as heat rushed over her, through her.

"Ohh, now there's something interesting." His amused voice was pitched low as he obviously caught the betraying color. "What's the blush for, kitten? Getting overheated?"

Turning from him, she pretended nonchalance as she laid the files on the table in preparation for the rest of the Pride's arrival.

"Kane, you're starting to irritate me," she told him coolly without turning back. "The cute little remarks are getting on my nerves. Keep it up, and I'll show you how a Feline really fights."

He grunted, the sound filled with sarcasm. "Be nice, Sherra, or I'll sic our little angel on you. She'll bite you, remember?"

Cassie had actually growled at her the day before when Sherra had snapped at Kane over something he said. The little girl was amazingly protective of him.

Sherra glanced back at Kane as she shook her head in pity. Poor Cassie. She was learning such bad habits from him.

"We promised to keep her away from you," she said. Kane was not a good influence on the child. "You're going to turn her into a little monster if you keep spoiling her the way you are."

He smiled with smug amusement.

"Beats the little doll you and Merinus would turn her into," he retorted. "Let the kid be a kid, dammit. It's not like she's had much chance in the past two years."

That was no more than the truth. From Dash Sinclair's reports, the little girl had lived through a nightmare of constant attacks and desperate flights as her mother fought to keep her safe. She was the first known Wolf Breed child to be conceived outside a test tube, and the price on her head was astronomical. But that didn't mean Kane had to turn a perfectly sweet child into such a little tomboy.

"She's a little girl, not a ruffian." Sherra turned on him with a frown. "Kane, you had her in a mud fight yesterday. There is no excuse for that this late in the year."

He smiled. A slow deliberate curve of his lips as his blue eyes filled with glee. "I know. Damn, that girl has good aim, doesn't she? And it wasn't that cold, it was warm as hell and she was having a good time. That's all that was required."

Kane and Cassie had both been covered in mud from head to toe. The minute Sherra had stepped out the door, berating Kane for the mess, a blob of the gooey earth had spattered against the side of her head. The little angel, once known as Cassie Colder, had informed her quite ferociously that she was a wolf and Sherra was a cat and if she wasn't very nice to Kane then she was going to get bitten.

"At the rate she's going I'm going to have to put you both on a leash," she told him heatedly. "Stop encouraging her. She's just a child."

In a second his expression went from smug laughter to intense, dark sexuality.

"A leash, huh?" His voice turned velvet rough, his gaze dropping to her breasts as they rose beneath the cotton T-shirt she wore. She could feel her nipples hardening. "Can we include handcuffs? I have some, you know."

Heat erupted between her thighs. Damn him and his teasing. He was only stoking the progression of her heat, making it harder for her to fight. And he was going to insist on making it worse. Could the day get any worse? she asked herself sarcastically.

"Only if you're the one in them," she snapped back, trying to ignore the image of him chained to her bed, straining beneath her as she lowered herself on the rigid length of his erection. The vision was too tempting to allow for long.

Unfortunately, her caustic words had little effect on him. Her insults rarely gained her so much as a glimmer of irritation within those dark eyes. But it did gain her the scent of hot, aroused male.

She could smell his lust now, like the rush of a sudden thunderstorm slamming into her senses. His eyes glittered, his expression darkening with hunger. If she looked lower, she knew that bulge in his jeans would more closely resemble a thick steel rod eager for release.

"That could be arranged," he murmured agreeably as he stepped closer, his heavy body moving with fluid grace and male power. "My room or yours?"

She was going to orgasm from the sheer intensity in his voice alone. Sherra felt her pussy flood with her juices, felt the hard ache of her nipples beneath the cloth of her shirt and wanted to hiss in fury. Why couldn't life, for just one year, be kind to her? she wondered in dejection. What had she done to deserve this?

"Only in your dreams." She managed to drag the derisive words past her lips.

He chuckled then. The sound was low, stroking over her already inflamed nerves as he moved closer to her. She wasn't about to retreat. If she did, he would only follow her. If he followed her he would learn just how desperate she was to keep as much distance as possible between them.

"You have no idea, baby. Want me to tell you a few of them?"

He paused before her, his broad chest no more than inches from her breasts. She fought to keep her breathing slow and even, but she was aware of the fact she was failing. As she knew he was. His head lowered as he watched her breasts rise harder before he lifted his lashes, staring back at her suggestively.

"No." She shook her head, trying to turn from him. She didn't need to hear about his dreams. The temptation of his touch was too great.

"My favorite one…" He ignored her denial as his hand moved, his knuckles running lightly up her arm. "…is the one where I have you stretched over my lap, turning your ass a bright pretty red for teasing me for so long. You squirming and begging for my cock each time I spank one of those rounded little cheeks. I would be more than happy to reenact it for you," he offered, with all appearances of polite consideration.

She should be outraged. Instead, Sherra stared back at him with shock and fought the clench of her buttocks at the thought of his hands descending on them in such a manner. Oh yeah, she could envision that one as well. Too well.

"That's quite all right, Kane," she sniffed with as much dignity as she could muster amid the overwhelming hunger rippling inside her. "You can just enjoy your little perversions alone. God gave men a hand and five fingers for a reason, you know."

"Hmm. I know. And I know for a fact just how well I can make those fingers fit my favorite little kitty, too. Come here, purr-baby, let me show you." Dangerous. Warning. His voice was like an addictive narcotic flooding her system despite the edge of fury she could see lingering in his gaze.

Cream flooded her cunt. She could feel it seeping from her vagina and slickening her labial folds with its thick essence. Keeping control wasn't easy to accomplish. Not when her tongue literally throbbed to share her pain with him and her vagina clenched in agreement. Damn him. She didn't need this right now.

It would serve him right if she gave him what he kept tempting her to. The rich potency of the hormone would be a fitting punishment for the months of arousal he had put her through.

"Kane. Sherra. No fighting today." Callan saved her from having to drag a scathing retort from her suddenly vacant mind when he walked into the kitchen, followed by his wife and the rest of the main Pride. "Let's get down to business and see if we can get something accomplished this time."

The last several meetings had been so unproductive as to make a mockery of his determination to ensure the Breeds a place in society. Not as a separate species, but as human beings deserving of life. That seemed to be the current debate waging among the inner circles of more than one government body.

"Okay, what do we have?" Callan asked as they all sat down. "Sherra, did you get those estimates?"

"Everything." She pushed one of the files to her Pride brother. "Farside does excellent construction work, Callan. I've researched every angle and they look like our best bet."

"I disagree." Kane did no more than she expected as he took his seat as well. He disagreed with everything she said lately. "It would require too many unknowns on the property at once and create a risk we don't need. That makes them more than untrustworthy, it makes them a hazard."

Sherra gritted her teeth for long seconds before she turned to him with a snarl.

"Farside Construction is one of the most respected construction firms in the nation. Their buildings have very high ratings for workmanship, they don't hire subcontractors and they make certain the work is of excellent quality from start to finish. Saying they are untrustworthy could be considered libelous, Kane," Sherra snapped.

He was once again being difficult. For some reason he thought it his job in life to make living an even greater hell for her than it already was.

Adrenaline pumped through her veins, making her insides tremble, her womb flex in need. Anger always made it worse. Made the heat spread through her body like a conflagration she had no hope of controlling.

"Settle down, Sherra. He said he didn't trust them," Callan reminded her as her gaze locked with Kane's. "We have to be certain who we're dealing with before we let them in on the property. Especially with Cassie here."

As though she didn't know that. She felt like hissing in sheer frustration.

"It's a meeting," she argued, turning to Callan. "I've busted my ass to get these files together and come up with the best choices for the work that needs to be completed. If he keeps shooting them down, we'll be building the damned houses ourselves."

"Which makes more sense, purr-baby," Kane sniped, his ever-present knowing smirk tilting his lips. "We have enough hands here and it's not like they weren't trained at damned near everything. What's the point in wasting money as well as manpower when we would be out no more than materials to do it ourselves?"

Irritation was beginning to thicken Kane's voice, as though he was growing tired of the ever-present battle between them. Which was too bad. He started it, his sniping and mocking comments continually battered away at her and she was growing sick of it.

"Because it takes away from the defense of the compound itself," she snapped back.

"Bullshit." He was frowning now, his dark blue eyes blazing. "You forget who head of security is here, kitten. Me. I know exactly what it takes to defend this compound and it doesn't nearly take two hundred Breeds at any given time to do so. Let your people do the work. It will build a sense of responsibility as well as pride in the home they've taken."

"You seem to forget the fact that most of those men and women you're talking about need a chance to rest and recuperate, not work their asses off all day." She planted her hands on the table, snarling back at him as she thought of the dull-eyed men and women who had been rescued from various labs over the past months.

"You can't coddle them like this, Sherra." He was nearly in her face now as the others watched in interest. "You're not going to help them by babying them as though everything was going to be just hunky-dory from now on. It's not. What they face isn't going to be a hell of a lot safer than those damned labs they were in if they're not careful. You can't let them think it will be."

Sherra could feel the blood suddenly pumping through her veins, her loins heating, her breasts tingling in response to the confrontation between them now. A sharp kick of arousal tightened her womb, nearly taking her breath as adrenaline surged through her bloodstream.

There was nothing so arousing as a fight with this man. She normally avoided it at all costs, but today... Frustration was like a rabid animal eating at her self-control. She was sick of his sniping. Sick of biting her tongue and keeping her mouth shut rather than pushing them both into something she feared she would regret.

"I'll be damned if I'll use them like slave labor, as you suggest," Sherra sneered back at him. "This isn't the Middle Ages and you aren't some petty dictator being allowed to take over."

Kane sat back in his chair, his eyes narrowing in anger as he watched her. She could feel his intent gaze, like a caress over her face, assessing her response. Seeing too much. He did that a lot, watching her like a damned bug under a microscope whenever they were in the same room together.

"So pay them a wage," he finally drawled mockingly. "No one suggested they do it for free. You're still going to come out ahead without the added danger that allowing others into the compound will bring."

"Enough, Sherra." Callan overrode the furious words getting ready to spew from her lips. She wanted to tear into Kane with a desperation that had her fingers curling into claws against the table. "You both have a good argument, but we have to come to a decision tonight."

"Good luck," Kane grunted sarcastically as he watched her. "Kitten here seems more determined to see us all dead at the moment then to have houses built."

Sherra felt a bead of sweat forming on her brow as he smirked at her. His eyes were dark, intent, watching her closely. She could feel him pushing her, knew he was and was helpless against the urge to fight back. She had to fight back. Had to show him she wasn't weak, she wasn't timid.

On the heels of that thought came the knowledge that her heat was what was actually pushing her. Instinct. To prove to him she was strong enough to take him, strong enough to fight by his side and challenge his strength, and the need to do so was becoming stronger. Daily, she could feel her own aggression surging in her body and it terrified her.

"He's irrational, Callan." She fought to sit back and relax as she glanced at the head of the table where Callan watched them both with a frown. "The man is so damned paranoid you'll be out there pounding nails instead of making decisions for the Pride soon."

"Give it a break, Sherra." Kane's voice was filled with impatience. "I need Callan to look after Merinus. You can't seem to keep her out of trouble."

Sherra turned back to him, incredulous at the accusation. Suddenly she had gone from coddling the exhausted Breeds to being unable to protect Merinus?

"Me?" she snarled, gripping the table in fury. "I wasn't the one who took her out on the motorcycle the other day. That was you. All I did was help her clean the stupid closet out."

"She almost fell on her head, dammit. I told you to keep that woman out of closed spaces. She's a hazard in them, didn't you pay attention?"

"I am not your sister's keeper!" she yelled. "How am I supposed to make sense of the crazy things she wants to do? She's your damned sister."

She was on her feet now, her finger pointing across the table in accusation as she faced him. She was sick of playing babysitter to an eight-year-old who knew more than she should, as well as a woman who didn't seem to know how to move her feet in a closet.

"Well, hell, excuse me, I thought you two should have enough in common to at least be able to walk and talk at the same damned time together," he drawled mockingly. "You should take lessons from her, Sherra. Being in heat the way you are, you should have the sense to at least pay attention when she messes up. You might want to learn from it."

She felt the blood drain from her face. Reality became limited to the dark, knowing depths of his eyes and the challenge sparkling there.

"You're insane." She tried to find the fury of moments before, but could barely manage to breathe past the shock instead.

He laughed, though the sound was mocking, filled with anger as he came to his feet and faced her with a tight smile.

"Am I?" he said. "Or do you think you can hide something else from me? Sorry, baby, I'm not nearly as stupid as you seem to think I am. And you want to know what else I'm aware of?" He leaned closer, his hands flattening on the table as he came almost nose-to-nose with her.

Her senses were filled with the scent of him. The smell of hot, furious male wrapped around her, nearly strangling her with hunger.

"What do you think you know?" she tried to snarl back, but her voice was weak, wary.

Now she understood the warning glimmer of anger that had burned in his eyes when she first entered the kitchen. Kane was flat pissed. And that was not a good thing.

"What I know," he said with brutal clarity, "is that you're in heat, Sherra. And I know who your mate is. I know, because it's me." He straightened then, staring back at her, seeming angrier at the knowledge than anything else. "Just like I know about the baby, the sterilization and your fucking stubbornness for the last few months. I know it all, and I'll be damned if you'll get away with any of it for even one day longer."

Chapter Two

You could have heard a pin drop was so clichéd, but it was the first thing that hit Sherra's mind seconds after Kane's furious announcement. She stood face to face with him, watching the muscle tic in his jaw, the flames that blazed in his eyes, and listened to the complete silence of the room. There were six others there besides them. Shocked, silent, watching her complete humiliation in stunned surprise.

Breathing harshly, she faced the man who had ripped her heart from her chest so many years ago, the man she had sworn to kill, only to learn her brother had nearly done the deed for her. She pulled her strength around her quickly, pride and pain and the determination that had helped her survive the years. Her head rose until she could stare back at him regally, making certain her expression was one of arrogant unconcern.

"Evidently, I didn't feel it was any of your business, Kane," she said shortly, pushing the words past her lips as she watched his anger grow. "Had I felt you needed to know any part of it, I would have informed you myself." She glanced meaningfully at Merinus before her gaze returned to Kane. "It would appear I didn't think you were on a need-to-know basis."

She was very well aware of who had most likely spilled the secrets she had fought to keep. Merinus loved her family more than anyone, with the exception of Callan and their unborn child.

Kane's lips curled back from his teeth in a silent snarl that would have done a Feline breed proud. "Guess again, kitten," he snapped. "I don't give a damn what you think I should or should not know. I gave you a chance to come to me, a month's worth of chances, and you hid instead. Now you can face the consequences."

Her laughter was mocking and brief. "Face the consequences? Sorry, Kane, I've made that trip already. It was a lousy one. I won't pay again. Now if you'll excuse me, I have better things to do. Callan can let me know what you decide about Farside Construction. I really don't give a damn how you handle it."

"Walk away from me and you'll regret it." His low warning had her halting the turn that would have allowed her to do just that.

She glanced over at him, seeing the determined cast of his hard expression, the raging fury in his dark blue eyes. She allowed her lips to lift in a bitter smile, let her gaze rake him coldly. "Regret it, Kane? I only wish I had done so the first time. I would have been so much better off."

She let her gaze encompass her family then. Those she had been raised with, the two who had come into it through their matings with her brothers. She saw their disbelief, their sympathy and shock.

"Goodnight, guys. My portion of the entertainment for the night is over. Maybe I can do better tomorrow."

Anger burned in her, warming her cheeks, trembling through her body as she let them look their fill.

"Do you think it will be that easy, Sherra?" Kane's voice was rough, the fight for control throbbing in his voice. "Do you think for one damned minute I'll let you get away with this?"

"I really don't think you have a choice." She stalked from the room, head held high.

She really didn't give a damn what he thought she could or couldn't do. She had endured eleven years of physical hell, of emotional pain, of fighting to make sense of why her body was betraying her, why she needed so desperately yet her flesh rebelled at any other man's touch.

Learning the reason why hadn't helped her emotional strength. To know it was a mating rather than a hunger, a bond that, so far, remained unbroken hadn't helped. Callan was already furious that she hadn't told him about the physical problems she had experienced earlier, that she had dared to attempt sterilization to ease the pain. His disappointment in her had shamed her more than she expected.

As she left the kitchen, she heard her brother's voice arguing with Kane, Merinus pleading. The others, of course, were commenting. She didn't care. They hadn't lived the past eleven years in her skin. Hadn't hungered with no idea of why, needed and ached for a touch that was never there.

She grabbed the banister of the stairs and began to race up the steps. The need for escape throbbed in her veins, pounded in her heart.

"Sherra." His voice stopped her at the landing.

She stopped, nostrils flaring as she breathed in roughly, her teeth clenching as she fought to keep from screaming. Turning slowly, she looked down at Kane.

Her body trembled in hunger. Her mouth watered with it as her tongue throbbed, the glands at the side aching to release the hated hormone. It was bad enough it was making her crazy, but she knew damned good and well what would happen if Kane ingested it.

The chemical reaction hadn't been as strong in Callan and Taber as it had been with their mates. If it held to pattern, it would be worse than super Viagra when it hit Kane's system. The thought of that had her pussy weeping in sobbing need. Like an entity with a mind all its own, it seemed to howl silently in protest of her refusal to allow it ease.

Kane was too damned handsome, tall and strong, the perfect male with tight, well-conditioned muscles. He was lean and humming with sexuality. His dark hair was cut short, his lashes shadowing his cheeks as he watched her.

She didn't answer him, merely stared back at him coldly as his lips quirked with knowing hunger.

"I'll be up later. Don't make me come looking for you."

Her jaw nearly hit the floor as he turned his back on her and re-entered the kitchen. Don't make him come looking for her? she thought incredulously. The son of a bitch, she was going to kill him.

Narrowing her eyes she moved quickly to her room. She changed swiftly into formfitting black pants and a snug sports shirt. She clipped her utility belt and holster around her hips, strapped the dagger to her thigh before tucking her hair under the black baseball cap, and snuck from the house. Let him come looking for her. He might get a hell of a lot more than he bargained for.

* * * * *

"Aren't you afraid of pushing her too far?" Taber asked politely several minutes after the rest of the family had left the kitchen and returned to their respective rooms.

For once, he wasn't with his new mate and wife, Roni. Rather, he watched Kane with those eerie green eyes of his, just a hint of censure showing in their depths.

"Aren't you afraid Roni's going to find out about your decision to keep her family away from her?" Kane came back at him, his voice equally polite. "I don't tell you how to handle your mate, Taber. Don't try to tell me how to handle mine."

Taber's lips lifted in a snarl, showing the dangerous canines at the side of his mouth. Kane smirked mockingly.

"It looks sexier when Sherra does it. Don't bother trying to intimidate me, cat boy. I only go easy on you because you're prick enough to take offense and I don't really want to take the time to scuffle with you."

Kane moved lazily from the chair, picking up his coffee cup as he headed for the full pot and, hopefully, the patience to deal with Taber. Of all the Breed males, Taber had to be the most temperamental. And Kane figured it was just his luck that this one decided to try to step in and berate him for his behavior with Sherra.

"Scuffle with me?" Taber growled. "You make it sound like a wrestling session. I could take your throat out, Tyler."

"You could try." Kane poured his coffee and fought back the weariness dragging at his mind.

He had been awake, it seemed, for months. The arousal was growing nightly, leaving him sleep-deprived and patience-worn.

When Taber said nothing else, Kane turned back, lifted a brow in question and waited. The Breed males could be unpredictable on the best of days, and though they did an admirable job of not resorting to violence, he was aware the potential was there.

Taber shifted, staring off for a second, his shaggy black hair falling over his face before he swiped it back carelessly and turned back to face Kane.

"I was there when she realized you weren't coming back. I was there when she lost that kid and when she nearly died," Taber snapped. "You weren't. I'm sick of seeing her hurt because of you, Kane. Lay off her."

"Go back to your mate and play kitty tricks," Kane retorted, growing angrier as the other man watched him. "Do you think I can't imagine the hell she went through, you purring bag of mismatched genetics? Do you think there's a chance in hell I'm going to let her continue to torture the hell out of both of us because of her damned stubborn pride? Get a clue, Williams. Not any longer."

Taber's body shifted dangerously, his eyes glittering with jade-colored fury as a growl rumbled in his chest.

"You're a smart-mouthed bastard, Tyler. Count yourself lucky you're Callan's brother-in-law and Sherra's mate, or I'd kill you for that."

Kane snorted. "Don't let that stop you from trying. I'm sure Merinus would forgive you pretty quickly." He set the cup on the small island counter, gearing for battle. He'd just as soon kick this arrogant panther's ass than look at him right now.

"Let up on her, Kane," Taber ordered again. "You don't have to stay on her ass so much."

"I have yet to get on her ass." Kane smiled tightly. "And when I do, you won't be invited to watch. Unlike your other brother, I'm not exactly into an audience nor do I need any help."

Tanner's sexual practices were getting out of hand, but no more so than Kane's libido was. If he didn't get Sherra into a bed fast, he was going to go certifiably insane.

"This isn't about Tanner," Taber reminded him furiously. "It's about Sherra. And I'm warning you…"

"Don't make that fucking mistake." Kane's voice lowered dangerously. "Don't even attempt to warn me of shit, Taber, because that's where we'll fight. She's my woman, my mate, my business. Stick to your own and stay the hell out of mine."

"You're killing her." The growl was becoming deeper, harsher. "I won't let you continue this, Kane."

"I dare you to stop me," Kane sneered. "I'll kick your cat ass all over this kitchen, Taber, if you even try."

"All right, children, break it the hell up." Roni stood in the doorway, her hands propped on her curvaceous hips, her blue eyes snapping with anger as she glanced at her mate. "What the hell is wrong with you two? This is not the time for this."

"Roni, this doesn't concern you," Taber warned softly as Kane shook his head, his hand rising until he could pinch the bridge of his nose irritably.

"Lord save me," he muttered. "Is the moon phase in the wrong fucking place or something? Some kind of weird Feline male PMS?" he asked Taber confrontationally. "Man, mating has not chilled your ass out any."

He was pushing the other man and Kane knew it. He knew it and refused to back down from it. He was sick of the growling, the snarling and the resentful looks he was given, more often than not, from the other man.

"Taber!" Roni was nearly screaming as she grabbed her mate's arm a second before he jumped for Kane.

Kane let a slow, cold smile shape his lips.

"Let him go, Roni. I'll deliver his pelt later."

"Damn you, Kane, shut the hell up," Roni yelled as Callan, Merc, Tanner and several others rushed through the other side of the kitchen, coming to a surprised stop at the scene that awaited them.

"What the hell is going on here?" Callan asked softly, his voice rumbling, his amber gaze less than pleased.

"Hey, Garfield, your brother here figures he can order me back from my mate since he's a happy little purr-boy with his own. Perhaps you should advise him otherwise." Kane leaned his hip against the island counter, though he watched the furious panther carefully. "I simply let him know he could kiss my damned ass to hell and back because it's not going to fucking happen." He directed his less than polite comments to the growling panther in question.

Roni had placed her body in front of her mate's, a death grip on his arms now.

"Callan, do something." She turned to the Pride leader at her mate's low order to release him immediately.

Kane watched his brother-in-law from the corner of his eye, saw the strain in the other man's face, the indecision. Tanner shook his head and mumbled something beneath his breath that had Callan glancing at him sharply.

"Kane, let it go," he finally said meaningfully. "Just walk away, man. For all of us."

There was weary resignation in Callan's voice, a sense of sadness that had Kane's own instincts kicking into overdrive.

"Why?" Kane asked him softly. "I won't let her go, Callan, any more than you'll ever let Merinus go…"

"Callan didn't destroy Merinus," Taber fumed with primal fury. "I won't watch you rip her apart again, Kane. Get the hell out of here and off the compound until this eases for her. Now, before they have to carry you out."

Kane bared his own teeth now. "You better hold him tight, Roni," he told her softly. "Because I just may have to teach your little kitty some manners."

Kane couldn't understand his own sense of rage any more than he understood Taber's, but it was impossible to miss the murder in the man's eyes when he set his wife aside and rushed him.

Pivoting, Kane moved immediately to meet him when the others jumped between them. Tanner and Merc grabbed Taber, restraining him as Roni's voice raised in alarm and Callan stepped in front of Kane.

"Enough." There was no anger in Callan's voice, no resentment. He watched Kane compassionately instead. "Bloodshed won't fix this, Kane. Fighting won't fix it."

"She's mine," Kane snapped.

"And for this reason, I've stood aside, just as Tanner and Dawn have stood aside as we've watched Sherra suffer since you've come here," he said just quietly. "For Taber, the battle is harder. You see, it was Taber who found her lying in her own blood as she miscarried. It was Taber who heard her tears, what may have been her dying words had he not acted as quickly as he did. It was Taber, Kane, that she begged to allow her to die because she could not face life without you or your child. And it was Taber who swore vengeance for her. You can't erase eleven years of pain, fury and hatred merely because it was a misunderstanding."

Kane stared at him in shock before his eyes swung to the piercing, furious gaze Taber had leveled on him. His hands clenched and unclenched, his jaw bunching with his own agony.

"I love her," he said, his voice tight, his chest aching with this new information given him. "I always loved her, and your threats won't change that. Neither will your hatred. Just as it won't change the fact that I'm not leaving and I'm not letting up. Every damned one of you might as well get used to that."

He stomped from the room, his own anger, his pain, overwhelming. His need to watch Sherra, to just know she did indeed still live driving him, pushing him... Destroying him...

Chapter Three

Escape was her only alternative. Sherra knew that staying in the house that evening would mean only one thing—an eventual confrontation with Kane that she had no hope of winning. And losing, at this point, wasn't an option.

Dressed in the dark, formfitting assault gear worn on patrol, she made her way through the compound to one of the few single houses that had been set up over the months. Tanner and Cabal had taken the small house themselves after Merinus happened to catch them involved in one of their favorite games. In the living room of the main house, nonetheless. On the expensive couch Merinus had chosen herself for the room, the two men had been eagerly convincing one laughing, highly amused Breed female to join them in play.

Since his rescue from a particularly sadistic lab, Cabal had, in his quiet, charming way, drawn several of the compound's females into his bed, where Tanner often joined them. Tanner, always the wildest of the main Pride, had taken to the ménages like a cat to cream. He and Cabal seemed almost an extension of the other as they charmed the young women into their bed.

For a while, Sherra had actually worried that her adoptive brother and Cabal were far closer than what she considered necessary. Learning the truth hadn't been any easier to take. They didn't have a liking for each other so much as they simply enjoyed making everyone crazy.

Sharing their women, convincing them to take on two Bengal Breeds rather than one, and immersing themselves in the sexual exploits had become so frequent that Callan had finally ordered them from the main house. To which Tanner had merely laughed and taken the newly built house instead.

As she neared the house, she cocked her head, listening carefully for sexual activity. Not hearing anything, she gripped the doorknob, stepped in and stopped in shock.

"Do you have a problem with bedrooms?" she asked, spying the mattress on the floor and the trio still presently joined in the center of it.

The female Breed was either sleeping or unconscious, who knew, sandwiched between Cabal and Tanner, one leg lifted over Cabal's who rested at her back, his cock embedded in her rear as Tanner eased slowly from her drenched, bare pussy.

"Do you have a problem with knocking?" He ran a hand over his sweat-dampened chest as he collapsed on his back, breathing roughly.

His poet's face, dark and arrogant, was relaxed with sexual fulfillment, his long black hair, striped with natural gold highlights falling to his shoulders and framing the masculine perfection maturity was bringing to his face.

On the other side, Cabal eased slowly from their partner, grunting at the obvious tight grip around his softening erection before he too lay back, relaxed, replete. His hair was gold with deep, midnight black streaks running through it. As striped as Tanner's was. It was like looking at two halves of one person. Their features and body build were nearly exact, their deep voices amazingly similar. Sherra often wondered if they didn't share blood as well as women.

She stared at the woman, now curled on her side as Tanner flipped the sheet over her nudity. He might ride them to exhaustion, relish them to their last orgasm, but he was highly protective of them.

"So lock the door or something," she snapped, moving into the room to close the door from prying eyes. "Callan is going to kick your ass if he finds out you're fucking his guards again, Tanner. And if I'm not mistaken, your little cat there is presently assigned to house detail."

He cocked one eye open, a charming, knowing little smile tilting his lips.

"Who's going to tell on me?"

She frowned, fighting to keep the amusement from her gaze.

"Keep disregarding orders and I will," she warned him, her voice hard, though she knew it would never happen.

Tanner had enough fun for all of them. He often reminded her what they were all fighting for with his laughter alone. He was cheerful, optimistic, and always found a way to enjoy life.

Cabal was quieter, more introspective, but always at Tanner's side no matter the prank or sexual exploit they were pulling.

"No, you won't." Only Cabal would dare to call her on it, just as he did as he rose from the mattress, unashamedly nude as he moved to the kitchen. "Want a beer?"

"No," she snapped, admiring the flex of his ass as he walked. She couldn't admire Tanner's ass, hell, he was almost a brother to her, but Cabal knew how to walk and she didn't mind looking. She might very well love Kane 'til her last breath, but that didn't mean she was blind. And a woman would have to be blind not to notice that fine piece of ass flexing in front of her eyes.

"Kane will kick his ass if you keep watching it like that, Sis." Tanner chuckled as he moved to his feet and pulled on a wrinkled pair of boxer shorts before flopping back on the couch. "That wouldn't be fair to him."

Sherra grinned unashamedly as Cabal walked back into the room.

"She staring at my ass again?" He tossed Tanner a long-necked bottle before twisting the cap off his own and flashing her a wicked smile. "Shame on you, Sherra."

"Whatever." She crossed her arms over her breasts, frowning at both of them as they watched her in amusement. "I need a favor."

"Uh-oh, now we're in trouble," Tanner sighed.

"Oh shut up," she grumped. "I just need you to find a way to keep Kane busy tonight. He's insisting on pulling me back to the house and I don't need a confrontation with him right now, Tanner."

"No, you need to be fucked," Cabal interjected, his gold eyes watching her soberly. "Stop running from him and you wouldn't have to ask for favors."

"I'm going to kick your ass if you don't shut up," Sherra snarled back at him. "I didn't ask for advice, I asked for help. Yes or no."

"No." Cabal frowned right back at her.

"Yes." Tanner flashed her a smile and a wink as Cabal growled in irritability.

"Dumb move, Tanner." He lifted his beer to his lips, tilting his head to drink deeply before sitting the bottle on an end table.

He bent, pulling a pair of jeans from the pile of clothes on the floor and pulling them over muscular, well-developed, incredibly gorgeous legs. Only Kane's legs looked better. But, she reminded herself again, she wasn't blind.

"Let her have her fun for now." Tanner shrugged. "Kane will take care of the situation eventually. I have faith in him."

Unfortunately, Sherra suspected he was right.

"Just keep him busy." She sighed, ignoring the byplay. "And keep this up…" She waved her hand at the still sleeping Breed female, "and the two of you are going to end up mated to the same woman. What the hell are you going to do then?"

Cabal smiled slowly. "One Breed, one mate. Remember? Don't worry, sweet thing, we'll grow up one of these days."

She doubted it.

* * * * *

The night was her friend. Sherra moved along the mountain above the Breed estate later that night, once again thanking the demon twins for their part in keeping Kane below as she scanned the darkness now, searching the mountain for any anomalies. She often took for granted the clear view she possessed in the darkness. It may as well have been daylight, despite the lack of light that came from the moonless sky. She found comfort in the darkness. A place to hide and attempt to make sense of the growing demands of her body.

The demands Kane was making were even worse. She fought the growing awareness inside her on a daily basis. Fought her need to touch him, not in hunger or in lust, but just to assure herself he was there. That he lived. That he breathed. She fought it to the point that she feared even the lightest contact between them because it was growing harder by the day to deny the fragile bond between them she could feel forming within her soul.

The cold was more than welcome now. The crisp, sharp edge of the temperature helped to clear her head, to hold onto her defenses. She could endure the temperatures better than the rest of her family could. Though she didn't have the pelt that the Snow Leopard possessed, she did have a tolerance to cold weather that the other Breeds didn't. The heat surging inside her could have had a lot to do with it, though.

The mating heat was worse than she had ever known it to be. As though Kane's presence had somehow stoked the fires hotter inside her. Her tongue was swollen now, the glands at the sides engorged, pulsing with the need to release the rich hormone contained within them.

It shocked her, the knowledge that she was displaying some of the characteristics that the males were showing. Her mate wasn't a Breed. The aphrodisiacal hormone would drive his sexuality higher, as it would hers. She closed her eyes at the thought. Doc Martin had warned her it would be like pumping Kane full of aphrodisiacs, making certain he was able to perform often enough to ensure conception.

The thought of Kane with a perpetual hard-on was more than she could cope with. Hell, he kept one now for the most part. Every time she saw him, his eyes glistened with arousal and the bulge in his pants seemed to get bigger. Tempting her. Oh Lord, how he tempted her.

She licked her lips as she worked her way along the mountain. She remembered clearly the steely hardness that rose from between his thighs. The shape and length, the thickness of the flesh, the feel of him. She wanted to groan in need at the remembered taste of his come pulsing across her tongue and down her throat. Or the feel of him thrusting between her thighs. Her pussy wept at the thought of that one.

Sherra gritted her teeth and kept moving. She would be damned if she'd give in to it. She could just see Kane, as dominant and domineering as any Breed ever born. He would turn into the same type of monster both Callan and Taber had turned into.

She snorted. As though she would ever survive being confined to that house amid the danger growing around them. In the past two weeks there had been three attempts to breach the outer perimeters of the security fence that ran around the mountain. They had yet to catch whoever had attempted to break through the security, though. Sherra couldn't imagine hiding within the confines of the estate during such a time. Callan and Taber had both lost their minds in their attempts to protect Merinus and Roni. It would make her crazy.

She couldn't hold back her regret that she couldn't conceive, her grief at the loss of the child she had once carried. Her womb flexed warningly, a prelude to the hard spasms that she knew would come soon—her body's demand that new life be created, that conception be allowed. She had destroyed any chances of that with her own ignorance years before. And she was growing so tired of fighting Kane and the heat building within her.

He was her mate. She had known that since learning the true depth of the bonding between Merinus and Callan. It didn't make the situation any easier to handle. To know he was the only man she could allow to touch her, to hold her, did not bode well for her future.

"Can you get any more stubborn, Sherra?" Kane's voice snapped into the comm link at her ear, causing her to tense as she paused on her way up the mountain.

With a silent curse she flipped the field glasses from the top of her head over her eyes and activated the pinpoint locator. She prayed he was in the communications building rather than heading up the mountain. Damn. There he was. She watched his unique locator as it moved steadily closer to her. The other Breeds on patrol were pulling back, giving him clear room as he made a beeline for her.

"I probably could," she grunted in frustration.

She could feel anticipation rising in her now. As though his voice had triggered a switch that let her body know he was coming near. Her breasts were suddenly sensitized, swollen again, the nipples poking against the material of her tank top as she paused and sat down on a large, moss-covered boulder. It wouldn't do any good to run from him. He was amazingly persistent.

Sherra breathed in deeply, catching the faint trace of his scent as he neared her. Her eyes closed in response to the sudden rush of blood that began to thunder through her veins. He smelled delicious, dark and exciting, his lust lending a dangerous edge to the heated smell.

He would be hard, she thought with a sigh. His cock would be pressed tight against his jeans, daring her to release it, to take him as she needed. She shook her head at the thought. Her self-control was running low. Lack of sleep and the building heat were starting to take their toll on her.

Sherra flipped the mic to the comm link away from her face, cutting off the others from anything she would say. The headphones were still in place, though, and she was able to keep up with the other guards as well as the communications center. She pulled the glasses off as she saw Kane's pinpoint marker coming steadily closer. He knew where she was. The small receptor pinned to the back of her jeans allowed her to be tracked easily by the computerized glasses that the Breed security force wore. She tucked the glasses into the pack on her utility belt and waited for Kane. The winter night was suddenly filled with a sultry, evocative warmth that seeped into her bones and made her want to relax into the touch she knew Kane would be eager to give her. He might be madder than hell, but as he entered the boulder-strewn area where she sat, his lust wrapped around her senses like a lava-hot wave of hunger.

"I didn't take you for a coward, Sherra." The first words out of his mouth had the hair at the back of her neck prickling in fury. She was unable to contain the low growl of anger that vibrated from her chest.

"There's a difference between cowardice and indifference, Kane," she snapped as she crossed her arms over her chest, watching as he drew closer. "I'm not frightened of you in the least. Now why follow me up here? Anything you have to say could have gone through the comm."

"Really?" he grunted as he stopped inches from her. "Do you really want the rest of the Pride to hear me tell you just how hard I intend to paddle your ass for leaving like that? And how far I intend to have my dick buried up your slick cunt while I do so?"

She would have been insulted if the sudden image that shot through her head didn't have her pussy pulsing in response instead. Pulsing? Hell, it was throbbing like a raw, open wound, begging to be filled. But that didn't mean she had to let him know that.

"Oh, aren't you brave?" She lifted a brow disdainfully. She would be damned if she would go to the trouble to actually get pissed off. Like she needed the blood rushing harder to her clit, carrying the faint traces of the hormone that escaped the glands in her tongue to the rest of her body faster. "You know, Kane, I could claw your eyes out easily. I'm a Feline. Remember?"

He grunted sarcastically. "I'll pretend to be your wolf and eat you then," he sniped. "Spread out."

Her arm moved before she really put any thought into it, her hand aiming for his face. Remarkably, he caught it a second before impact.

"You are out of line," she spat furiously. "I'm sick of your sniping and your veiled insults, Kane."

"And I'm damned sick and tired of being tied physically and emotionally to a hellcat who doesn't have the sense to take care of herself," he snarled back. "Do you think I haven't learned just what you've gone through over the years, Sherra? How bad the heat gets and the lengths you'll go to in denying it? You could have found me at any time."

Rage glittered in his eyes now. The deep blue flashed with fury as his lips tightened with it. It excited her, infuriated her.

"Oh yeah, I was really going to do that." She jerked her arm back, her body tingling, her heart aching from even that touch. "Come crying to you fresh out of that compound, believing you had betrayed me to begin with. I was just going to march right up to your door and ask you prettily to fuck me and make it easier. Even if I had known what the heat was, there wasn't a chance in hell of that happening." Keeping her voice low, keeping the rage tempered behind a harsh growl was one of the hardest things she had ever done in her life. She needed to scream, to rage, to strike out and hurt him as badly as she had been hurt when she believed he had deserted her.

"You knew I wouldn't just walk away from you, Sherra." He wasn't backing down. He was right in her face, the heat of his anger and his lust wrapping around her like invisible chains as his hands gripped her arms. "Damn you, you knew I hadn't betrayed you."

His flesh burned into hers. She could feel each individual finger, every cell as they came into contact with her body and became inordinately sensitized. She fought to drag in enough air to clear her head, to reinforce her self-control, but all she could smell was Kane and hot male lust.

Sherra stared at him, drawing in the scent of him, intoxicated by the sudden, overwhelming need to touch him. She was trembling with it, she realized. He was staring down as her as though he wanted to shake her senseless. His eyes were narrowed, thick lashes shadowing his cheeks, his usually sensually full lips pressed into a thin line of anger. And she wanted his kiss.

Her tongue throbbed as she strained away from him. She could taste the hormone spilling into her mouth as the engorged glands began to fill and demand the sharing.

"Get away from me." She tried to pull back from him, to deny the need and the hunger sweeping through her, and the rage that lingered just under the surface. "If you had cared you would have taken me with you as I begged you to, Kane, but you left me instead." Even she was surprised by the guttural sound of her voice, the harsh unbidden pain that echoed in it.

"God, do you think I don't hate myself for that enough, Sherra?" His eyes were bleak, filled with his own pain, his own regret. "Do you think I haven't literally prayed to go back and do it differently? To make sure you got out of there?"

He released her, as though he couldn't bear to touch her any longer. His hands pushed through the short strands of his thick hair as he blew out a ragged breath. He was fighting for control just as much as she was.

"Look, Kane." Sherra moved back, fighting to breathe past the emotions ripping through her and pouring off him. "It's too late to go back, and too much has happened to go forward…"

"The hell it has," he growled, staring back at her implacably. "Do you think I searched all these years, Sherra, risked my life and my family's and drove myself insane so you could wave me away as though none of it fucking matters?" A harsh laugh echoed through the night. "I don't think so, baby. And I think you know it's not going to happen as well.

Otherwise, you wouldn't be running like a scared little cat in the opposite direction every time I come near."

His voice had risen, but even more, he had moved. Sherra backed away, realizing she was retreating a second before she bumped into the boulder behind her.

"I'm trying to be sensible," she snapped. "Something you aren't, Kane. You have no idea what could happen. You don't know how it will affect you…"

"I know how you affect me," he growled. "I know my cock is like steel in my pants ninety percent of the time, I'm so hot to get inside you. I know every time I see so much as a scratch on your flesh I want to take someone apart. A bruise makes me rabid. I know whatever the fuck happened in that lab that night, I've never gotten over it. I've never forgotten. And, by God, I never gave up. You gave up."

"I accepted." Ragged, hoarse, her voice reflected all the pain and rage of the past years. "And now it's your turn, Kane. It's time to accept it's over. It was over the night those bastards raped me… Oh, God." She pressed her hand over her mouth as she watched him pale, watched the pain that washed over his face.

Pushing herself violently away from the boulder, she moved far enough away from him to avoid his touch, to breathe in the sultry night air rather than the bitter tinge of his pain.

She barely remembered that night. It had been hazy, misty. The drugs had reacted against the hormones that were surging through her system. The scientists had no idea the mistake they had made until she began going into convulsions beneath the bastard raping her.

"Sherra. I would give my own life to have saved you from that," he whispered behind her. "And that's the God's truth."

She shook her head with a sense of fatality. "No, Kane. You nearly gave your life, anyway, and we never knew it. It wasn't your fault. I don't blame you for it." And she didn't. She merely accepted it. "I'm not the girl you loved then. The girl who loved you doesn't exist anymore. She died with the child she lost. All that's left is the killer." She couldn't allow anything more. "I'm a Breed, Kane. Nothing more. Nothing less. And I'm in heat. It's physical. It's biological. And we have no idea how it could affect you. I'm not willing to risk it."

She could feel him behind her as though the heat of his body were a physical caress in and of itself. Then he was touching her, his hands sliding down her arms, stealing her strength with his touch as she heard the whimper that left her lips.

His touch.

Her breasts were so sensitive they ached, the flesh of her arms transmitting each calloused inch of his hands directly to her straining nipples, her engorged clit.

"I'm a strong man, Sherra," he whispered, his breath caressing her neck as she felt his head lower toward her. "I've lived when I wanted to die without you. I fought for you, even when I thought you were dead. Do you really think it's just biological? That any force short of death will keep me out of your body, keep me from fucking you until you're screaming for me to stop."

His voice echoed with the building, blinding lust she could feel ripping her insides apart.

Oh God, just once, she thought, weakening. To feel him inside her, stretching her almost painfully, fucking her with deep, hard strokes, his cock spearing inside her…

"Kane, please…" she whispered the plea, desperation thickening her voice.

"I'll please you, Sherra," he growled. "I'll please you until you beg me to stop. I swear. Here. Now. Wherever, however you want me."

His lips touched her neck, wrenching a cry from her soul as she felt the pounding, burning need racing through her.

"No!" She jerked from him. "I won't let you do this to me again. I won't love you, Kane."

A short, sarcastic laugh escaped him. "You must take me for a hell of a fool, Sherra." He shook his head, surprising her with the edge of amusement in the sound. "You're good, baby. So good, I think you may have even fooled yourself. But you haven't fooled me. Think about that. And start counting the days. Because I'll be damned if I'll let you run much longer."

Chapter Four

As though she had any intention of obeying any command Kane Tyler gave, Sherra thought, still more than furious later that night after joining the mountain patrols above the estate.

He hadn't ordered her back to the house. Not that it would have done any good, and he appeared smart enough not to try. She was thanking God he hadn't. Her body was rioting, the very fact that she now knew he was aware of the physical arousal seemed to only make it worse.

Too many celibate years, that was all it was, she assured herself as she moved among the trees, aware of the soft silence of the night, the caress of it upon her senses. It reminded her of Kane. Everything reminded her of Kane.

Touch me, Sherra. His voice had stroked her like the softest breeze as her hand gripped his erection, causing her flesh to electrify with pleasure. He had been iron-hard, hot and thick. A cock that would have pleased even the most discriminating woman. And it had more than pleased her.

She shivered, her pussy clenching at the thought of how well he had pleased her in the labs. Moving inside her, his body had been tight with the effort to control the need to rush to his own release as he drove her higher in hers.

Stop, she ordered herself as she breathed out roughly. Remembering would do nothing but make her weaker, hungrier. She couldn't afford to get any hungrier.

"Sherra, we have undeclared movement coming in east of you. Are you secure?"

Tamber Mason, a small, shy female Lion Breed, spoke over the communications link with an edge of tension as Sherra stilled against the broad base of a tree.

"How close?" Sherra kept her voice low as she checked her watch. It was a little after one, hours after having slipped away from Kane's threat.

"Less than a quarter-mile, moving in a diagonal line along the three o' clock marker to your location. A slow progression on a current heading that leads them directly to the back gates of the main compound." The link clicked several times as the channel continued to update to assure security as Tamber spoke.

Sherra pulled her weapon easily from its holster, checking the clip quickly as she moved into a stalking position. Her body fluid, ready for whatever threat she would come across, she began to move quickly to the location.

"Keep me updated on heading and distance," she murmured into the link. She pulled the night field goggles over her eyes and slid the transparent radar display into place.

Two small dots popped immediately into a small map on the peripheral of her right eye. Her own in blue, the undeclared heat source in red. She eased along the mountain, keeping low, easing through the dense underbrush and thick foliage as she headed for the intruder.

Undeclared meant Tamber had checked each link taken out and locations of the Breeds that were supposed to be on the mountain. There was one more pinpoint of movement than there should be, with no confirmation of the same location from the guards she had hailed before checking with Sherra.

"All I'm picking up at present is the one anomaly," Tamber said quietly as Sherra moved in closer, keeping a wary eye on the green fluorescent display of the goggles that now shielded her upper face. "But this one showed up out of nowhere. One minute we were clear, the next he was there."

Trusting the other woman to watch her back, Sherra noticed several blue displays moving in from other locations as well. Skirting a stand of shoulder-high boulders, she continued to move toward the anomaly, keeping a careful eye on the small red point as it slid along the map, coming ever closer to the gate that led into the main compound. It, too, was heavily guarded, which made no sense. It would have been easier for an intruder to gain entry from many other points rather than the back gate.

As light as a breeze, she slid through a thick stand of foliage, ducking easily to escape the upper branches which would have alerted an experienced tracker to the fact he was being stalked.

Council or fanatic, it didn't matter, they just kept trying. The attempts to gain entry into the compound seemed to worsen with every news report that slammed the airwaves. Some of the insinuations in those so-called reports were more than insulting, they were downright dangerous. Keeping up with them was next to impossible and counteracting them was becoming harder by the day.

And they kept trying. The attempts to kill the new human species seemed to grow daily. Moving slowly closer, Sherra eased past a stand of young pines and moved behind the intruder slowly. When she had him in sight, terror slammed hard and heavy in her heart.

"I wouldn't." She aimed the automatic weapon as he was preparing to lift the long, cylindrical missile launcher to his shoulder.

He froze for a long second. She smelled the fear radiating off his body just as she could sense his determination for murder.

"So much as shift and your head comes off," she snapped. "Tamber, alert the fucking house. We have a missile launcher."

She had no idea if she could take him out before he shot that missile off. His hand was on the trigger, the weapon nearly in place for a direct hit at the house.

"Evac, Tamber. Evac." Sherra gave the order to evacuate the house, listening distantly as chaos erupted in the control room.

"Is it worth dying for?" she asked the assailant, seeing his hand tighten on the trigger. "I can arrange it, buddy, if you don't lay it down now."

"Abominations..." His hand tightened.

Sherra fired immediately but the missile's trigger caught before he went down, causing the missile to launch.

"Incoming! Incoming!" she screamed. "God, clear that house out now! Now!"

She knew there hadn't been time to evacuate the house, no way to get everyone to safety. She ran to the fallen man, aware he wasn't quite dead. Instantly straddling his back, she ignored the blood dampening his shoulder and his scream of pain as she wrenched his arms back and secured them with the steel cuffs before jumping to her feet.

"Get that bastard," she yelled at two of the men as she heard the explosion farther down the mountain. "The rest of you are with me."

"Tamber, report," she yelled into the link as she raced down the mountain. "Goddammit, report!"

She could hear screaming in the background as orders were relayed, but no Tamber.

"No strike," a voice suddenly called out in her ear as she nearly stumbled down the slope, coming in view of the house. "We have no strike. No strike. Missile fouled."

Or something had fouled it. The heavily forested mountain with its thick-trunked trees had saved their hides. Two wide, centuries-old oaks flamed at the base of the mountain from the impact that had triggered the explosives in the missile. Breeds were rushing around the yards, pulling hoses from the hydrants located around the property to put out the flames before it set the entire mountain on fire.

"Check for others," Sherra snapped into the link as she turned and rushed back the way she had come.

She would kill the bastard.

As she neared the two Breeds dragging the screeching figure down the mountain she allowed a hard feline snarl of fury to pass her lips. They stopped, dropping their burden and standing aside as she stepped closer.

He was sobbing. Like a child caught at some indiscretion that he knew would bring punishment. The bastard wasn't even repentant, just terrified now.

"Hello." She whispered the word with a dangerous, predatory growl as she hunched down, knees bending to stare into the pale face. "What do we have here? A little midnight snack?" She displayed her teeth, seeing his eyes round at the sharp canines at the sides, top and bottom. She was one of the rare few with two full sets of the pointed weapons. Keeping the long canines hidden behind small smiles and a pretense of shyness hadn't been easy while living in the small eastern Kentucky town they had been hiding in before.

There was no need to hide now. She pulled her goggles back from her eyes, aware that they now shimmered eerily in the full light of the moon that glowed overhead.

He screamed a second before his eyes rolled back in his head and he lost consciousness. Sherra grunted coldly.

"Haul him to the cells." She stood up as she gave the curt order to the two guards. "I'm sure Kane and Callan are waiting for him."

Missiles now. She shook her head as she fought to breathe through the pounding of her heart. How the hell had he managed to get through their outer security and this far down the mountain before he showed up on radar?

"I need two more units out here. We need those outer fences checked as well as the security alerts," Sherra yelled into the link to be certain she was heard over the din in the communications room.

"On their way." Callan's voice was full-throttle fury. "Get your ass back here now. I need you here. We have wounded."

"Who?" Fear slammed in her heart at the thought of her family as she started down the mountain at a fast clip.

"The explosion caused flying debris to hit several of the guards and Merinus is in a tirade over you being out there. Get back here and calm her down. I don't need her having that baby before it's due."

Which meant Merinus was more than upset. Which meant someone close to Merinus...

"Where's Kane?" she breathed out harshly.

Silence descended.

"Oh God..." Her knees weakened in fear. Gathering her strength, Sherra raced down the remainder of the mountain toward the opened gate awaiting her.

She couldn't think, couldn't breathe. She refused to acknowledge the searing pain that gripped her chest and made her want to howl in misery. She ignored the despair, ignored the fear and ran with everything she had back to the house and to her mate.

"Dammit to hell, if you don't stop poking at me I'm going to break your fingers," Kane snapped at Doc Martin as he pulled a long sliver of wood from his shoulder, staunching the bleeding with thick gauze.

The flesh of his shoulder was a mess, raw and oozing blood, as Doc worked to clean the area.

Sherra stopped just inside the well-equipped medical room and stared at the wounds in horror. Smooth, perfect muscle bunched painfully as Doc inserted another injection of anesthetic to deaden the pain before pulling more slivers of wood from the flesh.

Wounds had never particularly affected her. She had been helping Doc for years with Callan's and often Taber's injuries. But seeing Kane, his perfect flesh torn and brutalized, made her stomach heave threateningly.

"Sherra, I need more bandages," Doc snapped as she paused behind him. "I already had to nearly sedate Merinus when she saw this, and everyone else is busy."

Rushing to the sink, Sherra hurriedly scrubbed her hands and arms down, rinsed and dried them before she rushed back to the gurney. Standing in front of Kane, she prepared the gauze, staring down at the utensils and the small metal bowl littered with wood fragments.

"Damned butcher," Kane muttered with a grimace as the probing began again.

He kept his head lowered, his shoulder hunched as though in pain, though she knew the area should be properly numbed by that point.

"It's pretty bad. He'll need a few stitches," Doc murmured. "You were lucky, son. Those flying splinters could have buried in a lung."

Sherra fought to control the sense of horror at the thought. Her stomach roiled as she swallowed tightly and prepared the sutures the doctor would need.

"You okay?" Kane asked her, his voice tense, his head still lowered.

"Fine," she said thickly.

She couldn't believe he was sitting there, that the attack had nearly taken him out. The fact that he was conscious and relatively unharmed amazed her.

"The others?" Her eyes rose to the doctor.

Doc Martin grunted in irritation as he worked another splinter free. "Minor. Limb clipped one of them. The other was thrown into a building. This one had the worst damage. If he would stay still I might manage to get the damned splinters out before next week."

Kane had shifted again, turning slightly farther away from Sherra. She frowned at his bent head. Was he hurt worse than he was letting on? He was acting so out of character that she moved until she was facing him, then bent down to inspect his bare chest for any wounds.

She froze in horror as his head finally raised and a sigh of resignation slipped past his lips. The scarring was horrendous. Long jagged lines of flesh extended from one side of his dark chest to the other. One sliced through a small male nipple, others criss-crossed his chest like a crazed map of violence. He hadn't had those scars at the labs. And she knew scars—these were old.

Dayan said he attacked Kane that night. That he should have been dead. Now I know why he was hurt so badly all those months that he was in the hospital, Sherra. They wouldn't let me see him then. But the wounds were terrible. Sherra remembered Merinus recounting the evil that had spewed from Dayan as he attempted to kill her and Callan's newly conceived child.

Kane's gaze was hard as he watched her. "Are you going to pass out too?" he asked her warily. "Merinus has already had her go at it. I don't think my shoulder can take another swooning female right now."

His expression was savage, his eyes glittering with pain and rage as she stared back at him helplessly. This had been the price he had paid for trying to save them. The scars he carried daily, a reminder of the deceit and betrayal which had infected her own family.

"Sherra, I need that gauze," Doc snapped. "Stop ogling that chest and hand it to me."

She jerked upright, aware of Kane slowly straightening as much as Doc would allow. She handed him the gauze, her mind a morass of confusion. She had never expected to see such scarring on the man she had come to think of as invincible over the past months. Her own anger and tangled emotions aside, she knew she had never imagined a time that she could conceive anyone actually wounding Kane enough to immobilize him. She hadn't completely believed Merinus until now.

She stood there, disbelief filling her as she helped Doc automatically. Handing him what he needed when it was needed, fighting the guilt and rage that filled her each time his muscles bunched. He didn't whimper or flinch, he endured the pain as though it were no more than an irritation.

"You didn't need too many stitches, but this wound is a mess," Doc said as he applied the last stitch. "You need to allow it to rest for a while. I'll change the bandages daily, give you a shot for the pain tonight and keep an eye on it. If it gets infected we'll be in for a battle. We don't want that to happen."

Kane only grunted.

Sherra stood silently as Doc gave him an injection for the pain, then bandaged the shoulder.

"Can you get him to his room?" he asked Sherra. "Everyone else is running around like chickens with their heads cut off. They'll let him get back in the fray rather than putting him to bed where he should be when this shot takes effect."

"I'll take care of it." She nodded firmly, meeting Kane's smirk as his head raised. Damn him, even wounded he had to be a mocking ass.

"He'll be pretty dazed until he goes to sleep. Stay with him." Her gaze flew back to the doctor as she began to prepare her excuses.

Was he insane? Stay with Kane? He was well aware of the effect that just being on the same property with him caused. He knew damned good and well what the same room would do.

"Don't you give me that look, girl," Doc snapped. "Someone has to stay with him and you're the only one here. Now get him out of here."

"Come on, kitten." Kane's voice was tired as he pushed himself to his feet, his other hand gripping the wounded arm. "Come tuck me in all nice and quiet and I'll let you go peacefully."

"Stay with him," Doc snapped again as Kane finished speaking. "No argument."

The world was just out to get her, Sherra decided as she pushed herself against Kane's side, looping her arm around his bare back.

"I want a damned bath," he informed her stiffly as they moved from the room. "I'm not touching my clean bed like this."

She sighed. Yes, the world was out to get her. She prayed someone, anyone, would be available to help him other than her. She moved him to the elevator and hit the button for the main floor where Kane had taken a room. Thankfully, it would open up not far from his door.

"Did you get the bastard?" he asked her as they entered the elevator.

"Yeah. I growled at him and showed some teeth. He passed out cold. I wish they'd at least send someone with backbone. These pansies faint if you smile at them the wrong way."

Kane grunted. He was leaning heavily against her as the doors opened, though, an indication that the painkiller was beginning to affect him.

"Let's get you to bed." She led him from the box and toward his room.

"Bath first," he reminded her as he breathed in deeply. "I swear to God, this day has been hell."

It was a new day, but she wasn't about to point that out to him. It was after two in the morning and dawn wasn't far away. She knew he was up before five every morning and usually still awake at midnight. He worked as hard, if not harder, than any of her family.

"Fine. Bath." What could it hurt? She would put him in the tub, wash his back for him and make sure she was there when he was ready to get out. No big deal. She knew Doc's drugs. They would make him a little dazed, kind of woozy, but he could stand up on his own.

She couldn't anticipate what was to come.

He couldn't unbutton the snug jeans. His arm was useless. Swallowing tightly, she unbuttoned them with trembling fingers, more than aware of the thick bulge beneath them. Keeping her eyes carefully averted, she eased them and his snug briefs down his powerful legs before he sat on the small chair beside the tub and let her unlace his boots.

Finally, gloriously naked and heavily aroused, he was able to step into the wide tub and lean back against it wearily. His head rested on the back, his eyes closing.

"You can't go to sleep, Kane." She was shaking as she watched the head of his cock bob along the tanned flesh of his abdomen. Only Kane would have a hard-on while he was half dead. It was just her luck.

"I'm awake," he muttered. "Just give me a minute."

He lifted his good arm, his fingers scratching lazily at his scarred chest. She followed the action, her eyes held captive by the thin scars, her heart aching at the pain they must have caused.

"He caught me outside the lab grounds," Kane said softly, causing her head to raise, her gaze to meet his.

His eyes were dilated and drowsy now.

"I'm sorry." She didn't know what to say. She didn't know what to feel.

"Bastard thought he could bury me and just walk away," he said softly, though his voice throbbed with anger and pain. "I managed to dig myself out and crawl through the brush. Some hikers finally found me. Half dead, fevered. They got me to a hospital, but I was pretty out of it by then. It was weeks before they were able to find out who I was. Months before I was coherent. By the time I was able to get help to you..." he swallowed tightly, "the labs were gone. They said everyone had died. Nothing was left."

He closed his eyes again.

She thought he had just walked away. She covered her face with her hands. Even after Callan and Merinus had told her what Dayan said, she still hadn't believed it. Not completely. Not clear to her heart. She didn't until now.

"I'm sorry," she whispered again.

He shook his head slowly. "Fuck it. Help me wash this grime from my body, Sherra, so I can at least sleep a while. I'll figure the rest of it out tomorrow."

Sherra felt her heart slam into her chest. Her pussy was screaming out in victory. Her hands were almost vibrating in pleasure at the thought of stroking his flesh, even with the barrier of a washrag against it. Slowly, she knelt beside the tub and lifted the clean cloth from the small basket hanging on the edge. Dipping it into the water she lifted the bar of soap.

"Hair," he mumbled, sitting up slowly and lowering his head. "Just use the soap. I do."

She washed his hair carefully, then after laying a towel over the bandage, rinsed the short strands with a dripping cloth. Removing it, she began to wash him quickly, desperate to get it over with and get him into the bed and hopefully sleeping. There was temptation and then there was desperation. She was passing desperation fast.

Her face flamed as he took the cloth from her and washed his hard, engorged cock and the sac beneath. His face twisted into a grimace of pleasure, the hard flesh jerking rapturously beneath his strokes.

"Enough." Her voice was strangled as she took the cloth from him and wrung the water out of it. She held out a towel. "You're squeaky clean and I'm tired of playing nursemaid."

A slumberous, sensual smile crossed his lips as he watched her through lowered lids.

"And you do it so well," he whispered, but forced himself to stand up.

Water sluiced over his tanned flesh as he rose before her, staring down at her, daring her as his engorged cock filled her vision. It was wet, water running in streams along the mushroom-shaped head and heavily veined shaft.

Sherra licked her lips, remembering much too well how good he tasted, how his groans of pleasure stroked her senses as her mouth had enveloped him. She swallowed tightly and quickly pulled the plug on the drain before rising to help him from the tub and towel him dry.

She thought she was strong enough to do it. She thought she could control the hunger and the need long enough to get him dry and in bed. But when she was once again faced with the thick length of his erection, she could only whimper in defeat.

His hands tangled in her hair as she knelt before him. He held her still, though there was no reason to. Her lips parted as the velvety head of his cock nudged against them, opened and allowed him to take her mouth with one smooth, shallow stroke.

"God. Sherra." His voice sent shivers cascading over her flesh as the thick, throbbing flesh filled her, stroking her swollen tongue as he moved his hips, caressing it as he thrust in and out with a strangled groan.

She whimpered, closing her eyes as her hands gripped his thighs and she began to suck at the engorged shaft. Just as he taught her a lifetime ago, her mouth closed on him, tongue stroking him, milking the sensitive head slowly.

His hands tightened in her hair, his body tensing as a ragged groan filled her ears and she felt his warm pre-come dripping to her tongue. It was salty, rich, making her realize how desperate she had been for his taste. She wanted it all, wanted to feel the hard hot spurts of his semen filling her mouth, coating her tormented tongue as he found his release in her.

"Sherra, baby." His voice was hoarse as he fucked her lips slow and easy. "Baby, this is so fucking good I could die, but I'm going to fall to the floor any minute."

To prove his words he nearly stumbled, a rough, tortured chuckle filling the air as she slowly released him. Looking up at him slowly, her breath caught at the stark male hunger in his gaze.

"Son of a bitch, I finally get my cock in that sweet mouth again and I can't even stand up long enough to enjoy it."

Sherra was shaking as she jerked back roughly, clamping her lips firmly shut as she stared at the moist length of male flesh. Dear God, what was she doing? She had lost her mind completely.

"Well, hell," he said roughly as he braced himself against the wall to stand upright. "Guess I can forget the release, huh? Can I at least get some help into bed?"

She shook her head slowly. He was watching her with heated intensity and a sexual hunger that made her body flame in awareness. This was madness, she told herself fiercely. She knew better than to think that this could ease her hunger for him. It would do no more than make it worse.

"Damn." She came to her feet, easing her arm around him and leading him from the bathroom to his bed.

"Yeah, curse for both of us," he growled as she jerked the blankets back on the bed and he sat down slowly. "Son of a bitch, no way I'm sleeping on my stomach with this hard-on, Sherra."

"You had it before I touched you." She frowned as he watched her with mild accusation.

"For you," he growled. "It's been hard since the night you stepped out of the shadows in Sandy Hook. Dammit, I can't even jack off enough."

She almost lost her balance at the roughly voiced protest. Then she did lose it as he lay down before pulling her to the bed beside him. Leaning over him, she stared down at him, alarm streaking through her system. Too close. He was too close now for her to maintain any sense of control.

"You need to go to sleep." *Please go to sleep*, she thought, *oh God make him go to sleep*.

But she couldn't resist touching the light stubble of beard along his cheek, her fingers glancing over it, the sensitive tips tingling in pleasure at the rough feel. He watched her, relaxed for a change. She had never seen him so laid-back, smiling at her easily, his eyes dark, filled with heat.

"You need to fuck me." He grinned suggestively, his dilated eyes nearly black now as he watched her. "Come on, just once. I promise I won't fall asleep on you," he wheedled in a dark velvet voice that sent electric flares of sensation tearing through her body.

How was she supposed to fight this new, suddenly gentle Kane?

Chapter Five

Sherra stared down at him in shock. He was teasing her? He never teased her. He either snapped at her or had something impossibly arrogant to say that was sure to infuriate her. He snarled at her, mocked her, called her cute little pet names and generally did his best to make her life hell. But he had never teased her so gently. So sweetly.

The time they had been together at the labs hadn't exactly given anyone an opportunity for laughter or for teasing. Life and death were a struggle, day by day. Each minute of their lives had been a lesson in death. How to accomplish it, either quick and silent, or with maximum pain. Sherra guessed she knew more ways to kill a man than most assassins walking around now. But she didn't know how to tease.

"Sherra." He reminded her of his request with a gentle, chiding voice.

Gentleness. He could be so gentle, so tender, that the thought of the single night he had given her brought tears to her eyes. She didn't want to remember, she needed desperately to forget. Remembering made her weak, made her ache for all the things she denied herself.

"You know I can't," she whispered, flinching as he caught her hand, watching her closely.

His calloused fingers smoothed over the back of her softer ones, creating a warming friction that had her breath hitching softly. She loved his touch. The heat and strength of his flesh always amazed her, as did the licking flames of hunger that grew in her womb.

"You always jerk like that when I touch you," he said, staring up at her somberly. "As though afraid I'll hurt you." His gaze was so dark, regretful. "Did I hurt you, Sherra, when I made love to you that first time?"

Sherra drew in a hard breath as he lifted her fingers to his lips. Hurt her? He had broken her heart, but physically he had given her more pleasure than she had ever known in her life.

She shook her head slowly, her eyes widening as his lips parted and he rubbed the pad of her forefinger against it. The sensation speared straight to her clit and from there to her aching pussy. His lips were firm and hot, full with sexual promise.

"Are you wet?" he asked her as his lips quirked in a smile. "I hope you're at least as wet as I am hard, baby. It wouldn't be fair otherwise."

His tongue swiped over her finger, causing her to jerk at the sensation. Wet, moist, she could well remember him stroking her clit with it as he held her thighs wide and sucked the little pearl to release. That hard knot of flesh swelled and throbbed at the thought as she fought back a groan.

Breathing roughly, she licked her dry lips, fighting to hold her eyes open, to make certain she watched every move he made. She wouldn't be able to bear it much longer. Having him touch her was a torment. An agonizing pleasure that she knew she would soon be helpless against.

"We have to stop." Talking was damned near impossible. She could barely breathe.

Hunger assailed her, filling her with the bittersweet pain of a lust she knew would never be fulfilled. She had made the mistake, albeit unknowingly, of condemning her body to bleak non-fulfillment. She wouldn't do the same to Kane. He had suffered more than enough already for daring to attempt to save her.

"Stay here with me, Sherra," he said, his voice low, vibrating with need. "Let me hold you. I'm too damned weak to force anything else on you right now."

He wouldn't have to. Her gaze trailed down his muscular chest, his tight abdomen and the rigid length of his cock rising up. She licked her lips nervously. She was so weak. As long as he was angry, sniping at her and appearing to hate her for her denial of him, then she could stay far enough away to keep her resolve. But this softer, kinder Kane made her hunger that much deeper.

Kane groaned. "Hell, baby. I want that tongue licking all over me, not your lips. Let me lick your lips." He pulled at her hand, drawing her down before the danger of the movement penetrated her mind, and she jerked back.

"No. I can't." Her tongue was throbbing, the glands swollen and desperate now.

Her breasts ached, her nipples hardening to firm peaks that rasped almost painfully against the snug fit of her top.

"Sure you can." His eyes were hot, glittering with dark hunger as he stared at the flesh of her upper breasts as they rose above the top. "Come on, baby. Let me kiss you again. I know how bad you need it. How swollen that pretty little tongue is. I could feel it on my cock, throbbing. Come on, Sherra, nothing's going to make me hornier than I already am."

He drew her down. Her head was screaming no. But every cell in her body was crying out differently. She could taste the soft mix of rainfall and sweetness in her mouth as she trembled in sudden fear and jerked away from him again, unconsciously swallowing the potent taste of the hormone.

She shuddered at the knowledge of how quickly the heat was progressing this time. She should have more time before the glands began to open up and spill their spice into her system. More time to prepare herself and make certain she could escape far enough away to keep him from knowing the hell she had yet to endure.

She moved back from the bed hastily. "I have to go."

"No." He leaned up on the bed, his gaze sharpening, his expression hardening. "Don't run from me like this, Sherra. Let me share this with you, if nothing else."

"You don't understand." She forced the words past her lips, a few more drops of the rich taste spilling from the glands. "You don't know, Kane. You can't understand."

"I understand I'm dying for you, and have been for eleven years," he said roughly. "Do you think I didn't make sure exactly what I could be letting myself in for when I found out what Merinus had experienced? Do you really think it's any fucking worse than this hard-on I'm packing? I could fuck you for weeks and not get enough of you. That piddling little hormone you put out isn't going to make it any worse."

He had no idea just how much worse it could truly get.

"You're crazy," she cried out roughly, her voice low. "You think it can't get any worse, Kane? You think arousal can't become a torture so painful you would gladly die rather than endure it any longer?" She looked down at him with bitter knowledge. "It can get worse. A hell of a whole lot worse. So bad your hips won't still as you try to fuck dry air. So deep and painful you're screaming in agony and you would fuck anything or anyone but you can't stand the touch of another person against your flesh. So debilitating you're useless in battle because all you want to do is fuck."

His eyes were black now, widening in shock as she described the past episodes she had gone through. His cheeks flushed a ruddy color and she could almost see his lust rising rapidly at the thought of such arousal.

"Then bring your ass down here and fuck," he snarled almost violently. "You know as well as I do that eases it, Sherra."

"Nothing eases it, Kane." She wanted to scream out her fury. "Don't you understand? Every time Callan fucked Merinus that hormone forced her to ovulate. Her body was prepared and gave her enough time to see if conception would occur before forcing her hunger again. I can't conceive. I won't conceive. Remember?"

"I could do without a dissection of my sister's sex life," he snarled. "And you don't know if what you're saying is true or not. All you have is supposition."

"And all you have is a hard-on," she sneered. "Jack off. At least you can find some relief there, Kane. There will be no satisfaction to be found in my body."

"I don't think so, kitty," he gritted out between clenched teeth as he came off the bed, stumbling for a second as his feet seemed to betray him.

Sherra watched, wide-eyed, while all six plus feet of furious, aroused male paused as though in confusion. His cock was dark and engorged, the mushroomed head damp with the pre-come that had seeped over it. He wobbled on his feet, the drugs affecting his coordination now. He stopped, stared down at them a minute, then started for her again and promptly stumbled again.

"Son of a bitch. I fucking hate drugs," he cursed.

Instinctively, Sherra moved closer to him, seeing the frustration and determination that was likely to cause him to end up on his ass. Not that she didn't think he deserved to be on his ass, but if he tore those stitches Doc would rip her a new one.

That was her first mistake.

His arms went around her, a wicked chuckle sounding at her ear, and before she could stop him, they were tumbling back on the bed.

"Oh hell," he cursed painfully as he came over her, catching his weight on his good shoulder, though he grimaced painfully with the jarring the wounded shoulder took.

Sherra stared up at him with a frown. Damned stubborn man. He was determined to have his own way, no matter what, and refused to listen to common sense.

"Kane, are you insane?" She didn't struggle against him as he moved between her thighs, his cock pressing against the mound of her pussy as her breath caught in hunger.

Kane's eyes closed for a second. Just long enough for her to watch the burning pleasure that streaked across his expression.

"Now what, big boy?" she asked him mockingly. Her clothes separated them and she knew damned good and well he was going to be out like a light before he could ever manage to get them off.

"God, you feel so good I could die right here and now and know nothing else has ever felt so good." His voice was hoarse with drugged weariness and thickening lust.

The words slammed into her heart. Sherra's eyes closed as she fought to block the sight of shattering bliss that crossed his face. His eyes had narrowed to pinpoints of dark heat as he pressed his hips into the cradle of her thighs. The hard length of hot, engorged flesh pressed firmly against her swollen clit, making her gasp in her own building ecstasy.

"Feel how good it is, baby," he whispered as his head lowered, his tongue stroking over the damp flesh of her collarbone. "Do you remember, Sherra? How hot and good it was that first time? Watching my cock sink into your sweet little pussy was the most erotic thing I've ever seen in my life."

The feel of his lips moving against her skin was heaven and hell. The pleasure was so exquisite her pussy clenched, pulsed, spilling her juices in a silky trail against the thin fabric separating her from Kane's eager cock. Her tongue throbbed with a pounding rhythm of need, spilling the sweet spice of the hormone into her mouth and sending it speeding through her system.

Oh, this was bad, she thought as her hips jerked against him in reflex. This was very bad.

Her hands gripped his bare flesh, holding onto his firm, muscular waist as he ground the heated shaft against her sensitive cleft.

"Kane." His name was a sigh of longing that she couldn't control.

Too many years of suffering the agonizing effects of the heat and not knowing its source washed through her. So many nights spent longing just for this, aching for the feel of his strong body covering her, his arms holding her, just as he was now.

"Shh, baby." He licked the rise of her breasts over the tank top. "Feel how good it is. Let me pet you, Sherra. All sleek and soft and hot against me. Such a pretty little kitty."

Despite the fever of lust building in her blood, Sherra snorted in amusement. "You're deranged," she groaned as she felt his fingers slide beneath the strap of the snug top and pull it off her shoulder.

"Mmm. Look what I found." He nudged the neckline lower with his chin, revealing the hard, distended nipple that rose pleadingly toward him. "A pretty little berry, all ripe and sweet just for me."

His tongue curled around it before she could steel herself for the action. She arched involuntarily, pushing it closer to his lips, a ragged wail of hunger echoing around them as she shuddered violently in his arms. Kane groaned roughly then slowly, heavily, collapsed against her.

"Kane?" Sherra swallowed tightly as Kane's head rested on her shoulder, his big body nearly crushing hers as all his weight lay against her. Comforting, but damned heavy.

"Kane?" She poked at his good shoulder.

His breathing was light and relaxed. He was growing heavier by the second.

"Dammit, Kane." She didn't know whether to laugh or cry as she began to struggle against his body, pushing against the unwounded side until she finally, mercifully, managed to roll him off her.

"Deranged," she muttered. "You're certifiable, Kane. Completely insane. You should be locked up."

weapons. But it wasn't handguns or rifles that he wanted to talk to her about.

"I'll be there in a minute. We need to talk," he answered tersely. He wasn't about to go into it on an open channel.

He'd awakened that morning with an erection that could have driven nails into solid oak, it had been so hard. His arousal had abated little over the course of the morning. If what Doc Martin had found was true, then the physical bond between him and Sherra had been there since that first night they spent together. How it happened, he really didn't care at this point. All he knew was the hunger for her and a need that had to be tenfold within her body.

He pulled open the door to the weapons shed and stepped into the cool, well-lit confines of the building. And there she stood.

Kane stared back at her as he closed the door, his teeth clenching at the signs of stress in her expression. Her eyes were dark with sleeplessness, her lips thin with the effort of fighting the heat that sizzled through her body.

"What the hell do you want, Kane?" she sniped instantly. "If you haven't noticed, I have work to do."

"Do you think you can fight this forever, Sherra?"

She flinched. If there was one thing that drove him crazy it was watching that betraying tremor of pain whenever she was forced to face something she wasn't willing to confront.

"Dammit, Kane." She drew herself up straight from the boxes she had been going through. "I have work to do here. I don't have time for this."

He strode closer, keeping his steps slow, non-threatening for now.

"Snapping and hissing as always," he said mockingly, allowing his lips to tilt into the sarcastic grin he knew she hated. "I prefer that sweet little purr you make when I touch you."

He needed her off balance. He had to shake that control she tried to keep between them.

"I do not purr." She looked horrified by the thought.

"Oh, yes you do." He watched her instinctive need to retreat, hiding his smile as she halted it, fighting to stand up to him, to best him. "You have the sweetest little purr when I touch you, Sherra. I remember it. Low and soft, resonating with pleasure."

His cock tightened, fully erect, harder than he could ever remember it being as he got close enough to smell the woman scent of her, to see the arousal she tried to bank glittering in her green eyes.

"You're insane," she snorted, turning, her hands shaking as she bent to the box, sorting through the straw as she pulled another new, gleaming automatic rifle from the depths and laid it with the others on the cart beside her.

"Am I?" He pulled her around to face him, feeling the feverish heat of her skin as she tried to jerk away from him.

"I'm going to kick your ass if you don't let go of me." She was panting.

Kane could see the fine film of perspiration gathering on her brow, the flush beneath her cheeks, the hunger raging in her gaze.

"You couldn't kick my ass if you wanted to right now," he retorted tightly. "Look at you, Sherra. You're weak, exhausted from fighting the heat, and nearly shaking with lust. How long can you fight it?"

"I've fought it before." She struggled as he pushed her against the low metal shelf behind her, holding her there with his body, his own carnal hunger beating at his brain with a strength he was beginning to fear.

"Not like this you haven't," he growled, gripping her hips as her hands braced against his chest. Her fingers flexed, nails rasping over the cotton of his shirt, caressing the mark on his chest with devastating pleasure. "Do you think you're alone, Sherra? Do you think for one damned minute that you're suffering without me?"

He jerked his shirt open, buttons scattering as she pulled her hands back.

"Look, damn you." One hand tangled in her hair as he forced her gaze to the mark a bare inch from his flat, hard male nipple. "Look what you left on me, Sherra. How well you marked me. Do you think for one fucking minute that damned hormone can make this harder on me?"

His voice was rough, enraged. He didn't know if he could hold back, if he could fuck her now without hurting them both.

He heard the small, keening sound of agony dragged from the depths of her throat as her eyes widened in pain and horror. Her face paled, her fingers reaching out to touch the reddened mark again.

Kane grimaced as pleasure, hot and destructive, raced straight to his cock. It swelled, pulsed, as he felt his pre-come seeping from the small, slitted eye in the center of the bulging head.

Drawing in a hard breath, he trapped her fingers against his chest, stilling them.

"I'm so sorry," she whispered, a whimper of need and denial that broke his heart.

"Sorry?" he asked her softly. "Oh no, baby. I don't want to hear sorry. I want to hear you purring while my tongue fucks so deep and hard up your tight little pussy that you scream with it. After I've eaten my fill of you, then I want to feel those sharp little nails scratching down my back as I fill you with every hard, aching inch of my cock. That's what I want to hear, Sherra."

Her eyes widened further, shock glittering brightly in her gaze as her head raised, her tongue flickering over her lips.

"Uh-uh." He shook his head, applying a bit of pressure to hers as he pressed her to his chest. "Don't lick those pretty lips, baby. Lick that mark you left me. Taste me, Sherra, before I do something we'll both regret."

His control was at its weakest point. His body was in full, overwhelming riot. His cock ached like an open wound and the mark on his chest was burning like a flame.

"Kane." She rested her forehead against him, her breath whispering over the sensitive brand.

Her hands clenched at his waist, holding tightly to him as she struggled for breath. Her small body trembled, nearly shaking as she fought both of them and the hunger raging between them.

Kane tightened his grip on the silken strands of hair at the back of her head before he flattened his palm, pressing again.

"Now," he groaned. "You know what I fucking need, Sherra. Give it to me before I take something you're not ready to give me."

The thin, desperate moan that echoed from her chest had him tightening, waiting. It wasn't a sound of protest or of fear, but of hunger. A second later his harder, male groan echoed around them when her tongue peeked over, swiping against the mark slowly, the slightly rough rasp tearing through his nerve endings and drawing every muscle to a breaking point as his head fell back, grimacing in an agony of sensation.

As delicately as a kitten, she tested the taste of his flesh, tempted the control he was exerting over the ravenous need rising inside him. She licked the hot little mark with a sensuality that destroyed him as she tasted his skin, each small caress making her move against him with more demand, the heat between them rising.

His jeans were a restriction he could no longer bear. With one hand at her head, the other moved between their bodies, his fingers struggling desperately with his belt as he fought to release his agonized flesh.

"Oh God! Kane, please..." Her hands were tight on his waist, her voice thin with denial and protest despite the hungry licks against his flesh.

"Sherra, baby." He jerked his shirt from his pants before returning to his fight with the belt. "God, touch me. I'm burning alive."

The belt came loose and a second later her hands were there with his, dragging open the snap to this jeans as he fought to release his cock. Her lips covered the mark she had made so many years before, suckling at it hesitantly, her tongue flickering teasingly now despite the mewls of protest vibrating against his skin.

A second later, he was free. Kane's rough shout of pleasure shocked him as Sherra's hand attempted to wrap around the thick stalk of flesh. The wounds to his shoulder were forgotten. Reality no longer existed. Kane could feel the blood pumping hard and heavy through his veins as pleasure became a firestorm, searing every cell in its wake.

Her hand moved on the sensitive flesh of his cock, flexing, caressing, driving him insane with sensations as he fought to hold back. He couldn't throw her to the shelf and fuck her like the animal he could feel rising inside him. But he wanted to. God help him, he wanted to taste the sweet juice he knew flowed from her pussy and then he wanted to fuck her. So deep, so damned hard she would never deny him again.

"Yesss…" He hissed out the word as he felt her moving lower, her breath moist and hot as she sought out each sweat-dampened area of sensitivity. Across his chest, down his abdomen. His cock throbbed eagerly. Lower…if he didn't get the bulging head of his erection in her mouth he was going to go insane. If he did get it in there he would go insane.

He groaned heavily when her tongue touched him. He could feel it, blistering hot and so damned good he barely restrained the release he could feel boiling in his balls.

"Damn you," he panted, lost in the haze of lust filling him, one hand gripping the base of his cock, the other tightening in her hair. "Suck it, Sherra. Wrap your mouth around my dick before I lose my mind."

But he was losing it anyway. He heard the small, strangled moan from her throat, felt it as he surged hard and heavy past her lips. His eyes opened as he stared desperately at the racks of weapons on the wall in front of him. He wouldn't look down. He wouldn't tempt his control…

Her hands were wrapped above his, gripping his dick, milking it as her lips, reddened and full, stretched around the engorged head. Her tongue flicked over the tight flesh, her moans rising as a small amount of pre-come ejaculated into her hot mouth.

He was close, too close, and she was pushing him to the edge. He shook in the storm surging through his body, the lust, the emotion, the need and pain that had built through the years. And he knew, no matter the demand of his body, this could never be enough. He could come in her mouth forever and he'd still be hard, furiously erect and dying for the liquid heat contained within the snug grip of her pussy.

His hands were hard, perhaps too hard, he feared as he pulled back, dragging her against him. He lifted her to the shelf that placed the honeyed entrance to her body in direct alignment with the rock-hard flesh aching to sink into her.

"Kane, no…" She whispered the words, but she was weak in his arms, her head falling back as his lips moved to her neck. "Don't do this. Please."

"Fuck it," he snarled, his hands framing her head, his gaze centering on her lips. "Kiss me, Sherra. Give it to me, baby. Now."

Her hands gripped his wrists, her lips trembled.

"I can't," she cried out weakly. "You know I can't."

Her eyes were nearly black with lust now, the hunger eating at her, destroying his control.

"Deny it's killing us both, Sherra," he snapped, lust and anger unfurling inside his mind until he didn't know if he should fuck her or spank her first. "Deny my right to this — to your kiss. Deny I'm your fucking mate, damn you."

She opened her mouth, whether to deny him or to agree he would never know. All he knew was the hunger, the rage, the need sending spikes of agonized demand through his balls and into the tormented shaft of his cock.

His lips covered hers, his tongue plunging deep. His woman. By God, his mate.

Chapter Six

The kiss destroyed her. Silent screams of protest, of fear, ricocheted through her mind, but her body, her flesh, ignored every wailing demand that she stop. His tongue swept into her mouth, a cooling relief against the fiery ache of hers, so tempting, so soothing she was lost.

Pleasure exploded throughout her body as she eagerly fought for control, joining him the erotic duel of lips, teeth and tongues as she inhaled his scent, tasted his kiss, felt his hands holding her to him, forcing her to acknowledge what she would have continued to fight. Her need. Her hunger. It raged and raced through her system, slamming into her mind, stealing her will and leaving her weak and shaking in his embrace.

It was like nothing she had known before. Even the first shattering kiss they had shared so long ago was only a weak imitation to this one. It weakened her, sent her senses screaming with the building heat that raced through her body, pooling in her womb and growing ever brighter.

A conflagration rose inside her as his lips and tongue combined to drive her insane with the ravenous carnality that slammed into her body. She couldn't fight him as well as herself. Not while his lips covered hers. His tongue tempted and stroked, driving her mad with the need to feel his lips twisting over hers, drawing on the swollen flesh of her tongue, relieving her of the hormone that now pulsed and throbbed within her swollen glands.

Years of need, of brutal demand caused by the very nature of what she was, rose to the surface. The battle for supremacy began then. His tongue tangled with hers, but this wasn't what she needed. It stroked and cooled the burning flesh of her own, but again, she needed more. She fought to push past it, to gain control, to attain the victory of having his lips enclose it, sucking it into his mouth, easing the torturously swollen glands that seemed to fill further now.

His hands were tight in her hair, holding her to him, though there was no longer any need. Her arms twined around his neck, holding him close, her nails biting into his scalp as sanity slipped further and further away.

Her craving for him built. His taste, his touch. It became a raging tempest, sweeping aside fears, objections and reason as incandescent heat exploded through her body.

With a victorious cry, she pushed her tongue past his lips and dissolved. Instantly Kane was there. His lips trapped her tongue, his mouth drawing on it. The hormone trapped within the swollen glands poured free as his hips jerked, his cock pushing hard and insistent against the damp fabric of her thin pants, the bulging head parting the lips of her pussy as it nudged in as far as the material allowed.

Sherra was trying to crawl into his body now. The rapturous pleasure spreading through her as Kane suckled at her tongue was nearly more than she could survive. Her cunt spilled its thick essence against the cloth-entrapped head of his cock. Her hands held him to her, her head falling back as he fought to gain every drop of the aphrodisiac from her.

In the back of her mind she knew the terror would come later. The fear for Kane and his safety would send her past every fear she had ever known. For now, though, there was only his kiss, his rumbled groans of growing male arousal, his cock rocking against her pussy, his hands pulling at her top, the pain easing in her tongue but growing in her womb.

Her eyes struggled to open as his head jerked back from her. A whimper escaped her, fear pricking at the heat building between them. His face was flushed, heavy with lust now, his eyes nearly black, dilated with the instant effect of the hormone absorbing into his system.

"Kane." She whispered his name with an edge of desperation as he forced her arms down then jerked her top over her shoulders. The spandex material stretched tight, trapping her, hampering her movements as her breasts cleared the edge of the straining fabric.

"Don't talk." His hands lifted the swollen mounds. "Every time you talk you think. Don't fucking think, Sherra, just feel."

"What have you done, Kane?" She shuddered as his tongue swiped over a hard, riotously sensitive nipple.

"What I should have done six months ago," he snarled, surprising her with the anger behind his words, the need that vibrated in his voice. "Damn you, Sherra. How did you survive this alone, baby? Sweet baby… If I don't have you I'll die from it now."

She cried out as the hunger became ravenous. His lips surrounded her nipple, drawing on it strong and deep as his hands tore at the waistband of her snug pants. His cock was throbbing, the head literally pulsing as it tried to bury deeper in her pussy, to defy the material of her pants between them, threatening to rip past the threads as her cunt heated destructively.

The hormone. Sherra whimpered as the pleasure screamed through her body. His mouth drew on her nipple, his teeth rasping, tongue licking, as the brutal fist of sensation tightened in her womb.

How would he function? How would she? The heat was pronouncedly stronger in her than it had been in Merinus. The agonizing pain would soon be ripping through her womb as her body fought to conceive. It was a useless void, and no matter how fertile the hormone wanted to make her, it could never support life.

The thought of the life she could never help create was shattered by his touch, though. He was out of control. They were out of control. His hands were hard as he fought to get her pants off her hips while keeping her locked to him, a hard, fierce growl tearing past his throat.

Kane held her secure, his mouth, teeth and tongue tormenting the hard flesh he held captive. Her nipple was becoming so sensitive, so enflamed that the pleasure was almost pain, pushing her higher as it overwhelmed her.

She could feel her heart racing, the blood surging through her veins as his teeth scraped over the pointed crest before gripping it gently, holding it captive as his tongue flicked over it with hungry demand.

Sherra twisted in his arms. She needed to be closer. She could feel the swirling mass of sensation growing in her womb, pulsing with a demand she couldn't deny. Not any longer.

Her upper arms were bound to her body by the taut fabric of the sleeves of her top, but her hand reached out, gripping Kane's muscular forearms as he consumed her breasts.

He drew the hard point deeper into his mouth, sucking it with strong, hungry movements as his tongue continued to flay it. She could feel each rapid flick of his tongue throwing her closer to oblivion. She was helpless to fight it. Helpless against it.

"Please..." she whimpered, but didn't know if the plea was for him to cease or to take her deeper.

Her head fell back as she gasped for breath, shuddering as his teeth raked the tender tip, sending white-hot flames licking from her breast to her womb until she convulsed in heated, agonized ecstasy. Her cries echoed around her as she tightened, shuddered, her nails biting into the hard arms she held as bells and sirens began to wail around her.

Sirens?

Kane's mouth released her nipple with a slight popping sensation as his head raised, a snarl drawing his lips back as Sherra suddenly realized the sirens were coming from outside. Warning, strident, the alarm system wailed through the compound, shrieking around them as the raised voices from outside the shed finally penetrated the haze of lust enveloping them.

Her gaze flew to his, her hands trying to reach for him as her brain processed the fact that there was now danger surrounding them. Danger to the occupants of the house, Cassie, Merinus and Roni and their unborn babes. Her mind fought to accept the sudden switch, the need to protect rather than to fuck, the need to fight rather than to touch.

The last thought was like a knife wound in her soul as Kane suddenly dragged the straps of her top over her swollen breasts and back to her shoulders and she adjusted the neckline. He was struggling for control himself. She could see it in the raging emotion glittering in his dilated eyes, the tight grimace on his flushed face as fury began to envelop him.

"I'll kill the fucking bastards!" Enraged, Kane forced the heavy length of his cock back in his pants. He hurriedly snapped the material together, jerked the belt closed, and grabbed one of the rifles from the wall along with a loaded clip.

He slammed the ammo in place, checked it and turned quickly from her.

"Kane." Grabbing her belt and holstered weapon from the shelf, Sherra jumped to the floor and rushed behind him.

"Stay put." He turned on her, his eyes blazing. "After I kill whoever dared set those sirens off, you're fucked, Sherra. Accept it and get the hell ready for it. Because I won't wait much longer."

Sherra stood still in shock as she watched him disappear out the door. Precious seconds were lost as she fought to make sense of what happened and Kane's sudden fury. The hormone.

A cry tore from her throat as she rushed after him, pulling her revolver from its holster as she reached the door to see the Jeep spinning from the small parking area in front of the shed. She jerked the communications unit from her belt and attached it to her ear as she raced for the other Jeep.

"Report!" she yelled into the mic as she flipped it to her lips.

"We have intruders." Tamber maintained control as she reported to Sherra. "The front gates have been breached. I repeat, we have a breach. All available units to the main compound. We have a breach."

Sirens were blasting as Breeds poured from the barracks and raced on foot or in Jeeps to the main gates where the long, black, stretch limo had managed to break through the barrier.

"Someone grab Kane!" Sherra shouted into the mic. "Callan, where the fuck are you?"

She was nearly in tears as she slammed the jeep to a stop, no more than a hundred from where the limo was surrounded. "Callan, damn you. Get Kane. Now. He's not rational. Callan, where are you?"

She raced across the distance as voices raised and positions were taken to surround the vehicle.

"Sherra, stand down!" Callan ordered her suddenly, his voice rough through the mic. "Stay back. Kane's in control. Get up to the house with Cassie. We need Merc out here."

She slid to a stop at the warning tone in Callan's voice. Her chest tightened with fear. Merc was the strongest of the Breeds. Six and a half feet, his body corded with muscles. He was also the finest shot in the compound. Trained as an assassin, so far no one could beat his aim. What the hell was going on that they would need Merc?

She turned for the house, meeting Merc as he tore from it, his rifle in hand.

"Merc." She slid to a stop, staring up at him, terrified. "Kane..."

"Get inside with Cassie, Sherra. Kane can take care of himself." He rushed past her, racing for the tower in the center of the yard.

The sniper's nest. Sherra gritted her teeth furiously as she ran into the house, only to be welcomed by Cassie's inconsolable cries as she wailed for her momma from Merinus' arms.

Several of the younger Breeds stood inside the room and crowded the hall, staring at her, looking for direction.

She switched the channel on the communications pack quickly, going straight to a private line to Tamber. Access to the line was given only to those highest in security.

"Tamber, what the hell do you see?" Tamber's position within the communications shed would have her in a position to see everything going on.

"We have the limo surrounded with no movement so far," she reported.

Sherra moved to one of the long windows in front of the door, watching the activity outside carefully. They were too far from the main gates to see exactly what was going on, but with over a hundred Breeds surrounding the vehicle, it wasn't going far. They were sitting ducks for Kane's fury.

"Get me a main line to Callan," she ordered. "This is priority one, Tamber. I have to talk to him now!"

Kane's control had been nonexistent when he tore from the shed; the hormone wreaked havoc on logic. Normally even-tempered, his control had been nowhere in sight when he left her.

"Main line...on..." Tamber responded as the low hum indicated the switch.

"Callan. Dammit, are you there?" She couldn't stand the fear whipping inside her.

"Hurry, Sherra," he snapped tersely in reply, giving her the go-ahead to claim his attention for valuable seconds.

She turned from the room, breathing roughly, rage and violence shimmering through her system.

"He kissed me, Callan," she told him quickly. "He wasn't rational when he left the shed, he may not be rational now. You have to get him out of there."

The silence was thick, discordant with the mechanical buzz of the unit as she waited.

"Son of a bitch, if his timing doesn't suck," he cursed.

Sherra couldn't agree more. But Kane had never used anyone else's idea of a schedule. It had always been his way, however he had to manage it. Just as he had done this time.

"Agreed," she snapped. "Now get him out of there."

A second later, Sherra tensed, her eyes widening as shots fired and all hell broke loose both inside and out.

"Cassie, no!" Merinus' frightened cry heralded a small bundle of determined energy as she threw herself out of Merinus' arms and to the door.

A youthful, enraged wolf's howl echoed through the house an instant before she evaded Sherra's grip, wrenched open the door and flew out into the sun-dappled nightmare awaiting her.

"Cassie's out! Cassie's out!!" Sherra screamed into the headset as she raced out the door, knowing she would never stop the child, never catch her before a stray bullet found her instead.

Chaos reigned outside. Breeds broke position, several jumping for the little girl who twisted, screaming, long black hair flying around her as the back door to the limo began to open.

Sherra's soul twisted in terror as the little girl rushed headlong toward it, her feet flying, her little body easily defying the men and women attempting to block her, to catch her before her blood marked them all.

But blood didn't flow. Cassie's body wasn't thrown back by the impact of deadly bullets. As the limo door began to swing open, the little girl threw herself headlong into the dark shadowed interior of the car.

The door closed quickly, ominously behind her.

* * * * *

Hours later, Kane could still feel the insidious crawl of the overwhelming terror that had filled him when he heard the screaming announcement that Cassie had escaped the house. At the same time, one of the younger Breeds panicked and set off a barrage of bullets as the door to the limo began to open.

One little girl. Over a hundred battle-hardened, animalistic warriors and no one had been able to catch her before she threw herself into the dark interior of the car a second before the door slammed shut.

Kane sat alone now, the scene replaying in his mind as the near consequences of her actions slammed into his brain. She could have died. Right there in front of his eyes, that precious bundle of energy could have died.

He came to his feet in a surge of energy, restrained, vibrating with violence as he jammed his fists into the pockets of his jeans, ignoring the flash of pain in his engorged cock as the material tightened further.

First, he had failed to protect his own unborn child and now he had nearly failed with Cassie. It didn't matter that the situation had quickly been diffused and the intruders had turned out to be Roni's irate half-brother, Seth Lawrence, and her long-lost father.

The Breeds could have whisked the intruders from the property, no one would have questioned it and then arranged a meeting outside the estate between Roni and her brother. That option was not feasible now. Cassie had ensured that.

"Cassie's still crying." Merinus stepped out on the porch, her voice soft in the growing darkness as Kane kept his back to her.

Kane hunched his shoulders against the guilt flaying him alive.

"At least she's alive to cry," he finally snapped, so damned angry at himself, Sherra, and an innocent child that he could barely make sense of anything else.

He could still see her running, her face tear-streaked, fear contorting her expression into a snarl as she launched herself through the men and women attempting to stop her until she disappeared into what could have been an enemy's arms.

"She's making herself sick, Kane," Merinus told him as she came close to him, leaning her heavily pregnant body against his side. "She's just a little girl. One who believes in herself enough to do what she feels is right. She knew there was no danger…"

"No, goddammit," he cursed roughly. "She didn't know anything of the sort, Merinus. She could have died…" He broke off, shaking his head as he moved away from her. "Hell. I died a thousand deaths when Sherra alerted us she was out there. Bullets ripping around like a damned war zone and she throws herself into an unknown vehicle. If I had anything to throw up I think I would have done it then."

He moved away from her. He had spanked Cassie. He shook his head against the knowledge. When he got her back in his arms he had taken her straight to her room, set her on her feet and spanked her twice before ordering her straight to bed. Then he had yelled at Sherra. Hard, bitter words that had ripped from his chest as he watched her eyes go blank with shock.

You were supposed to keep her fucking contained. Dammit to hell, there were four of you watching her. Couldn't one of you keep her contained for ten fucking minutes? He had thrown the words at her furiously.

"God, I'm a bastard," he muttered. "I'm not just an asshole, Merinus. I'm the worst bastard to ever walk. Someone should have shot me."

She sighed heavily behind him.

"You're human," she finally said softly. "I know about the kiss you shared with Sherra. I can imagine what you're going through without the burden of protecting everyone that you place on your shoulders, Kane. You can't protect us all alone. Shit happens. That's what you used to tell me. All you can do is be as prepared as possible when it unloads and get through the stink the best way you can."

He grunted at that. He was an arrogant ass to boot, it seemed. He stared around the darkened yard, the tall fence that stretched below the wood line, the guards patrolling the area. It was like an armed camp, not much better in its restrictions than the Council labs had been.

In the farthest distance of the main compound, lights blazed in one of the small guesthouses. Seth Lawrence, his father, and chauffeur were presently under close watch as Taber and Dawn attempted to convince Seth and Aaron Lawrence that right now, Roni wouldn't be told who they were or why they were there.

It wasn't so much that Seth Lawrence had disregarded all their requests that he wait before forcing such a meeting. It was the damned hairs at the back of Kane's neck. They prickled in warning, making his nape tingle with an itch that wouldn't go away. He had agreed with Taber's fears about not allowing the meeting yet. Roni's physical health had been precarious when she first came to the compound.

The length of time she had endured the mating heat, along with exhaustion, the sexual excesses and resulting pregnancy had worn her down. But that wasn't Kane's only worry where the Lawrences were concerned. The timing was off. Two mated females pregnant, the only known Wolf Breed child in existence living there with them, and now this.

"Hell. I saw Cassie running for that car and you know what ran through my mind, Merrie?" he asked her painfully.

Merinus sighed deeply. "That you had failed." She surprised him with that answer. "You couldn't protect your own, and now you hadn't protected Cassie either."

He turned to her slowly.

"Yeah," he breathed out roughly. "But how did you know?"

"Because it's the same thing Sherra told me before she locked herself in her room," she answered him gently, forcing him to embrace her as she moved into his arms.

She was another man's wife now. She carried a child, would be a mother and would face more danger than he could have ever envisioned. But she was still the little girl he had bribed with chocolate. The young woman he had held as she cried over the loss of her mother. The same who had called him an asshole for most of her life. He fought not to hold her too tight as his arms constricted around her.

He could smell baby powder and chocolate for just an instant. The scents that had been uniquely Merinus' when she was a child. A precocious bundle of energy that got into more trouble than seven men could keep her out of.

He kissed her forehead gently before pushing her to the door. "Go on in. You need to be resting or terrorizing Callan. Not out here messing with my head."

She didn't laugh as he expected her to, and neither did she go in the house.

"I get scared, Kane," she said softly as she looked up at him worriedly, her hands lying protectively on the mound of her stomach. "I'm scared for you. You can't go on like this, and neither can Sherra. I want our children to be safe, our lives to be led with some measure of peace. Until this thing between you and Sherra is resolved, that won't happen."

"Give it time, Merinus," he told her gently. "Go on inside. I need to take care of some things before I head to bed myself. I'm beat."

Sleep was the furthest thing from his mind, though.

"Good night, Kane," Merinus said softly. "If you get a chance, check on Cassie soon. She's devastated that you're angry with her. She's convinced she saved lives. And she's just a little girl."

She possibly had saved lives. His and the Lawrences. If it hadn't been for the alert that Cassie was speeding toward them he would have been in the line of fire when the bullets started flying. Only the alert and his attempt to intercept the little girl had saved his own life.

"I'll look in on her soon," he promised, steeling himself against the tears he knew he would see in the little girl's eyes and her plea for her momma.

"Merc and Tanner are leaving in the morning for Dash and Elizabeth's location. I'll place Cassie with Dawn if that's okay. I think they'll do well together," Merinus told him softly.

Merc and Tanner's absence would leave a weakness within the group as a whole. He could only hope the situation in California resolved itself soon.

"Dawn's a good choice," he agreed. "Hopefully we'll not have any more surprise visitors to push Cassie into such reactions. I still can't figure out why she pulled such a damned fool stunt."

"Because her fairy told her to," Merinus said worriedly. "And that, Kane, terrifies me. She's withdrawing too deeply into herself and this fairy issue. We need to talk to her mother about it when they collect her. It's going to get her hurt."

Or drive him over the edge of his sanity. Sherra already had him teetering. Cassie could well push him over.

"I'll discuss it with Dash as well," Kane promised. "Go on, I'll see Cassie soon."

He watched as Merinus entered the house, a dim shadow, heavy with child and rich with life. He shook his head before he followed her and moved quickly up the back stairs to Cassie's bedroom. Putting it off wouldn't make it any easier.

He opened the door to her bedroom, his heart clenching at the sight of her curled in the middle of the large bed, her blue eyes haunted as she stared back at him, tears streaking her face.

"Hey, pup," he greeted her softly as he moved and sat on the edge of the bed, looking down at her. "You want me to leave?"

She shook her head jerkily.

"I'm sorry, Kane." Her breath hitched with tears. "I had to save you. You can spank me all the time, but I had to."

Damn, she was going to be a handful when she grew up, he thought, stubborn as hell.

"I'm sorry I spanked you." He stared down at her, his heart breaking at the thought of the spanking he had applied to her rear. "You terrified me, Cassie. I don't know if I could have lived with myself if something happened to you."

She nodded slowly. "I know that, Kane. But that's what I think, too. I would always cry if you were hurt. And Sherra would too. She cries too much. Almost as much as I do at night."

He stared down at her in surprise. "How do you know?"

"'Cause I can hear her when the house gets all quiet and she goes outside on her balcony," she whispered. "Sometimes, it sounds like she hurts awful bad too, Kane. I think her heart is breaking like mine did, when I thought my momma couldn't save me from that bad man." The rooms were soundproofed for the most part, compliments of the Council. But Cassie liked to open her door the slightest bit that security blocks allowed. If Sherra were on her balcony, several rooms away, it would be easy for Cassie to hear her.

"I think you should tell her you aren't mad at her anymore, Kane," the little girl said solemnly. "You hurt her feelings really bad."

He had hurt more than her feelings and he knew it.

"Come here and give me a hug. I'll make sure Dawn gives you a cookie tomorrow. But that's it. One. You broke the rules."

She jumped to his arms, hugging him tightly and planting a loud kiss on his cheek. "My momma will be all done soon," she whispered in his ear. "And my daddy Dash will need me to go to him really fast so Momma will be happy. You have to fix Sherra, Kane. I don't want you to be all alone when I'm gone. My fairy worries about you."

He stiffened, watching as she snuggled back under her covers, staring back at him with eyes that were too old, too knowing.

"Cassie, about this fairy," he said hesitantly.

"You have your fairy too, Kane," she told him, her childish voice at odds with the knowledge in her eyes. "Sometimes I see her. She's got all this pretty dark hair that looks like a cloud around her face. It looks like Merinus' hair. And she has blue eyes, and she smells like real roses. Not the perfume kind. The real kind."

He stilled. Despite the fever that made him rush to Sherra, the danger he could feel moving closer and his own worries about Cassie, he couldn't stop the shock that filled his system. His mother had smelled like roses. The real kind. The very ones she so loved that still filled the backyard behind his father's house.

"Roses, huh?" he asked her softly.

"She'll talk to you if you let her," Cassie said softly, her eyes drooping with sleepiness now. "'Cause she loves you. Just like my fairy loves me…"

Kane rose to his feet, shaking his head in confusion. Damn, that kid could bring armies down if she tried. He drew in a deep breath, tucked the blankets around her snugly and headed from the room.

He had an appointment with his mate.

Chapter Seven

Sherra was able to hold back the pain until late that night. She knew it was coming. She had enough experience with the symptoms of mating heat to know what would happen.

After the explosive episode in the weapons shed, the rest of the day was so busy, so filled with the fight to survive that she was able to train all her senses on her job, rather than the increased arousal that began to build. But when darkness fell and weariness tugged at her body, it slammed into her harder than ever.

Her womb spasmed painfully. Life. She could feel her body screaming out for the life-giving pulse of Kane's semen spilling into her, his cock throbbing, swelling within her, spurting into her. She didn't want his fingers, she wanted his thick erection. She wanted all of him, coming over her, pinning her down, taking her with erotic fury.

She whimpered as she paced her bedroom, her flesh almost electrified, overly sensitive and in need of his touch. She had removed her uniform earlier, showered and dressed in the soft, lightweight cotton of one of the long gowns she preferred to wear. The tunic-style material fell to her feet, with long slits running to her knees and giving her freedom of movement.

The bodice ghosted over her breasts, rasping her nipples gently as the small straps over her shoulders held it in place. Between her thighs, her juices dampened the small panties she wore, almost making them useless. Her pussy was so slick, so wet, she knew it would suck Kane's cock to its very depths within seconds.

She closed her eyes as she curled up on the couch in her sitting room, her head cushioned on the thick armrest, her thighs clamped together. Her breasts were tortured, hard curves of radiant heat that had her nipples nearly popping through the material of the dark gown.

Her tongue was throbbing, swollen, and every so often she could feel and taste the pulse of the hated hormone in her mouth. Spitting it out didn't help, she had tried that before. There was nothing she could do but suffer through the nights and stay as far away from Kane as possible when it became so intense.

She should have stayed away from him last night and run hard and fast this afternoon. The memory of his cock tunneling into her mouth, throbbing against her tongue, so hard and hot, had her biting back a moan of overwhelming hunger. She would have sucked him to completion if he hadn't been so weak. She had been possessed, so hungry for the taste of his seed spilling into her mouth that she had lost her sanity. Instead, she had lost her control. She hadn't been any stronger that afternoon.

She hated this. She wrapped her arms across her breasts, drawing her body into a fetal position as she fought the need to go to him. He was her mate, her mind screamed out in protest of her denial. *Go to him.*

She shook her head. She wouldn't. She couldn't. The heat lasted a month for her—she had no idea how long it would affect Kane, what it would do to him. He had nearly died for her once. He put his life on the line for her family daily. She couldn't face the potential that he would be hurt further, in ways she could not anticipate.

Sitting up with a ragged groan she pushed her fingers through her damp hair and fought to push the thoughts of him out of her mind—the tanned contours of his muscular body, the thick length of his cock, his lips as they whispered over hers and his erection pushing inside her greedy pussy. His hands, holding her as he fucked her with hard, deep thrusts.

"Oh hell..." She cursed her hunger as an abrupt knock sounded at the door.

Raising her head she watched in resignation as the door opened and Kane stepped inside. Her eyes widened in alarm as she stared at the scarred chest, then lower to the rippling muscles of his abdomen and the straining length of his erection tenting the sweatpants he wore. He closed the door, clicking the lock in place.

"God, don't do this to me." She shook her head desperately as he pushed the gray pants over the straining flesh and down his powerful thighs.

"And watch you suffer instead?" he asked her quietly. "Suffer myself? The hell I will, Sherra."

She whimpered. "Please, Kane."

"Take the gown off." He advanced on her.

She couldn't breathe for the excitement. He looked savage, determined. His eyes glittered with lust, with emotion. Emotion hell, it was love, she knew it was love and hated herself and everything she was for what she was putting them through. Yet, she couldn't stop. If she stopped, she would splinter. If she gave in, the pain she had held inside for so many years would tumble free, destroying them both.

"I can't." She trembled as he came to her, standing before her, his cock gleaming with the pre-come beading at the tip.

Sherra licked her lips in hunger.

"What eases the pain, Sherra?" he asked her. "What makes it better?"

She shook her head. Nothing eased it, but she couldn't take her eyes off the glistening, mushroom-shaped head of his cock.

"Your mate's semen eases it," he told her softly. "Sexual release and my seed spilling inside you. I can give that to you, Sherra." He stepped closer as her lips parted involuntarily.

"I can't force you," he said softly. "I won't force you, but by God I'll make sure you're so hot you can't walk straight if you don't do it willingly. I won't let you run. Take the gown off, Sherra. Let me give you every drop of what you need."

What she needed was his cock shuttling hard and deep inside her, pumping into her in mindless orgasm, his seed filling her hungry womb with rich, potent heat.

"Kane…" she whimpered desperately as her tongue slowly ran over her lips, moistening them a second before the tip of his erection brushed them.

With a tortured cry she leaned forward and enveloped the head in her mouth, sucking it in, tasting the salty sweetness of his come on her tongue as it mixed with the potent spice of the hormone releasing in her mouth.

Ah, God. She worked her tongue over the hard flesh, greedy for every lick now, every taste, every ragged moan out of his mouth as she began to consume every inch pressing back to her throat. She wanted more. Needed all of him. Her hands gripped his hips as she suckled at him strongly, filling her mouth but still never managing to take the full length.

"Sherra, baby." His hands gripped her hair. "Oh yes, kitten, swallow my dick. Eat it all up, baby."

The explicit words flamed in her mind. Before, during the night in the labs, he had held back. She had sensed him holding back in both his needs and his words. He wasn't holding back now. He was taking her, showing her the man he was and the need vibrating in his body.

Sherra took the wide head deep inside her mouth, her tongue working on the sensitive underside as she tried to open her throat for him. He was thrusting in and out with long, controlled strokes, his breathing hard and heavy, rough amid the slurping, gasping sounds of wet hunger that spilled from her lips.

"Ah yes. Swallow it, baby." His cock was throbbing hard, pulsing against the back of her throat with each thrust. "Milk my cock with that pretty mouth. Come on, baby, take it. Take it all, sweetheart."

He was moving faster now, harder, his flesh swelling on her tongue as she sucked and licked with greedy abandon until she felt the first hot pulse of creamy fluid erupt at her throat.

His hands were tangled in her hair now, holding her close, sliding his cock as deep down her throat as it would go as he released stream after stream of hot, silky liquid down it.

Sherra swallowed desperately, tasting him on her tongue, in her mouth, filled with the excess of his release as he cried out above her.

When he pulled back from her still suckling lips he bent, gripped the bodice of her gown in both hands and ripped it from her body.

"Kane…" Her protest was filled with fear as he went to his knees, hands gripping her thighs and pulling her hips to the edge of the couch.

He stared down at the bare flesh of her mound, his lips swollen with passion, his eyes darkening as the lust built.

"I want to taste you," he whispered. "Like I did before, my mouth buried in your pussy, my tongue driving you to orgasm."

He would consume her. Panic flared inside her. She was so wet, so juicy from her need. That fluid contained the same hormone that spilled from the glands in her tongue, only less potent.

"Don't." She tried to jerk forward, a last weak protest before he could bend to her.

His eyes narrowed for long seconds, darkening further as she watched angry determination begin to build in his expression. He pushed her back until she reclined once again, moving closer to her, his cock aiming for the convulsing entrance of her pussy.

"For now. Just this for now." His voice was consumed with lust. "I'm not taking," he panted roughly. "I'm giving. See, kitten, watch me give."

Her eyes dropped to her splayed thighs, widening as the head of his cock parted the slick lips of her pussy.

"Kane…" She tilted her hips, drawing her feet up until they rested on the couch edge, opening her further, allowing her to watch as he began to sink into the blistering depths of her cunt.

"Look how pretty." His thumbs parted the pink folds until she could feel the head of his erection stretching the small entrance of her vagina as he began to push inside her. "The tightest, hottest little pussy I've ever been inside, Sherra. Suck me in, sweetheart. Just like you did with that pretty mouth. Suck me in as deep as I can go."

She held onto her ankles with a desperate grip. She couldn't touch him, couldn't allow herself that weakness. Her head rolled on the back of the couch, her hips writhing as he began to work his cock inside her.

"More." She was panting as he moved slowly, making her feel each inch of her tissues parting around the broad head.

She could feel the protest of unused muscles giving way to steel-hard width. The greedy wash of fluid eased his way into her, the throb of the satiny cock head as it forged inside the narrow channel.

"No." He was breathing roughly, taking her so slowly she was shaking, her hips jerking roughly as his hands clasped hers, holding them to her ankles. "You won't kiss me, won't let me lap at your soft little pussy, then I'll make up for it here." His voice was dark, so rough it stroked her senses like a firm loving hand.

He was killing her. Stretching her by slow degrees, making her cunt walls spasm and flex in rapturous greed as he worked slowly deeper.

"Damn, kitten, you're so pretty." His eyes were glittering, his face sweat-dampened, his thick lashes in damp spikes as he glanced at her. "There's nothing so sexy as watching your sweet pussy take me. Do you remember that, Sherra? Remember how sexy it was the first time? It's even hotter now. I swear, I think you're tighter than ever."

Sweat ran in slow rivulets down the sides of his face, along the scars of his chest as he suddenly slid into her to the hilt. Sherra bucked against him, strangling for breath as her cunt fought to adjust around the unfamiliar girth.

She stared back at him, whimpering at how deeply he filled her, needing him to take her violently, to slam his flesh as hard and deep inside her as possible.

"Please." She was almost crying with the need.

He smiled tightly. "I know how you need it, Sherra. I know what you need. Give in to me and you can have it now. Refuse me and you'll wait until I can't stand it anymore before you get it."

Her eyes widened. "What?" she wailed, her hips jerking, fighting for the friction she needed as he worked his hips in tight, hard circles, grinding the head of his cock against her grasping cervix.

"Just a kiss," he crooned softly as the knot of need tightened in her womb. "Give me your kiss, Sherra, and I'll fuck you until you're screaming because you don't know if it's pleasure or pain."

Her kiss. Her destruction. "Kane, don't do this to me." She could feel the tears welling in her eyes, her body out of control, her pussy spasming around his cock as he slowly slid it to the entrance again before sliding back slowly, opening her all over again. "Please. It hurts. It hurts so bad." She was crying and helpless to stop it. The punch strokes in her womb were killing her. The more he teased her, the harder they became.

His eyes fell to her abdomen, watching the hard convulsions of the muscles there each time his cock butted against her cervix.

"I'm sorry," she cried, emotion and fear overwhelming her. "I'm sorry, Kane. I can't. I can't give you what you want. I can't…"

He cursed. A low, horrible sound of bleak acceptance before he jerked free of her body. Before she could scream out in protest he pulled her forward then flipped her over, braced her against the couch and rammed home.

Her back arched as a scream tore from her throat. His cock was an iron-hard length of ecstasy plunging inside her now. His hands gripped her hips, almost bruising in their strength as he fucked her so hard and fast she swore he would batter his way into her womb. And she still needed more. She shrieked with need as she lunged back into each stroke, driving him harder, deeper, feeling her orgasm tightening in her womb with each thrust.

"Damn you." He bent over her, his fingers delving between her thighs. Locating the hard swollen bud of her clit, he began to rub it with firm destructive strokes as he raked the tender channel of her pussy.

She was dying. Sherra felt her body tighten, felt fire erupt in her cunt, her womb, then explode so hard and fast she could do nothing but wail within the storm overtaking her.

"Yes. Fuck, yes. Sherra. Come for me, baby. Yeah. Oh baby…" He was filling her. Spurting inside her as he continued to ride her through her orgasm, each thrust sending him to the very depths of her pussy where he shot a stream of thick, hot seed at the mouth of her womb before shuttling back then surging forward for another.

Her body was soaking it up. Her orgasm ripped through her, shuddering through her bones and leaving her weak, exhausted, as she lay against the cushions of the couch. The muscles of her pussy flexed, milked his flesh as he held himself deep for one last powerful spurt of release and collapsed over her.

"This won't work for long," he warned her, his breath caressing her ear. "You know it won't, Sherra. You need more than just the cock and hot seed. Your body and your mind need more. You can't deny it forever."

She shook her head, trembling at the ring of truth in his words. She would make it enough. If this were all she ever had, then it would be enough.

He moved away from her slowly, his softening flesh easing from the hold she had on it as he breathed out roughly.

"Are you okay now?" His hand smoothed over the curves of her butt.

She nodded quickly. She had to get away from him. Had to have a minute to figure out exactly what had happened and where she had lost every measure of common sense she possessed.

"Do you need more?" She could feel the hunger throbbing in his voice.

Her pussy screamed yes. Her head pleaded no. She shook her head, her fingers digging into the cushions of the couch.

"Fine." His voice was hard, bleak. "Be in the doctor's office first thing in the morning. I'll meet you there. You can hide from me all you want to, but I'll be damned if your health will suffer for it."

He was dressing. She could hear him behind her as she allowed her body to settle against the floor, her head resting on the couch away from him. She couldn't look at him, couldn't face what she had just allowed to happen.

"Damn you for being so stubborn," he finally cursed shortly. "If you need me, Sherra, you know where to find me." The blend of sarcasm and fury had her shivering in dread.

She had purposely never really pushed Kane in the past five months. Had let him make his smart-assed comments, let him torment her with his presence and his often-angry asides. But she hadn't pushed back. She hadn't pushed because she knew when she did she would trigger the dominance he kept such a tight leash on. The dominance she had just triggered with her refusal to share the heat with him. With her refusal to give in to the needs rioting through her body.

The bedroom door closed behind him as he left, leaving her naked, the tatters of her gown hanging from one shoulder, his seed weeping from her aching pussy. But the pain was gone. At least, for now.

Chapter Eight

Sherra stomped from the basement labs late the next morning after the intense examination and ritual bloodletting Martin was into. The man had to be part vampire to need all that blood.

Foregoing the elevator, she moved quickly up the short flight of stairs, coming out just beyond the wide front entryway and directly across from the kitchen.

"You promised." She heard Cassie's low forlorn voice.

"I know I promised, pup," Kane said softly, his voice drifting into the hallway. "But Dash and your momma had to move again. They'll call us as soon as they settle in. I promise, everything's okay, but we need to make sure they stay safe, too."

"But I need my momma," Cassie told him with irrefutable logic. "The fairy misses her."

Sherra sighed softly. Cassie blamed everything on the fairy, even her harebrained rush into the danger the day before.

"And the fairy has every good reason to miss her," Kane said gently, his normally rough voice velvet-soft. "They'll be heading home in a day or so anyway. I sent Merc and Tanner just to help Dash watch over your momma. I told them, no matter what, you stand in front of Cassie's momma, and they said they would. Do you think they'll let anything happen to her?"

Sherra tilted her head, her eyes closing as his voice soothed even her frayed nerves.

"No," Cassie said hesitantly. "Merc and Tanner and Dash will keep her safe. But I'm her little girl, Kane. She's supposed to tuck me in. And tell me when it's okay to eat my chocolate so I don't get a tummy ache..." Sherra's eyes flew open, her heart clenching at the sound of coming tears.

"Excuse me?" Kane adopted a tone of false offense. "Have you got a tummy ache yet?"

Sherra shook her head. They had kept chocolate strictly out of reach.

"Well, no..."

"And don't you get plenty of chocolate?" he asked her then, causing Sherra's eyes to narrow warningly.

"Yeah. Those Oreos are the best, Kane. Double chocolate." The sigh of bliss had Sherra staring into the doorway in surprise.

Surely, Kane was not slipping that child chocolate. He wouldn't.

"Good girl. So, what's your poison? Milk?"

"Yes, please. And four cookies this time," the little girl answered.

"Four?" Laughter filled his voice. "Double chocolate? I don't think so, my girl. Two double, or four normal. Your choice. And don't remind me that you aren't supposed to have more than one today. I might feel like I need to keep practicing how to say no to wily little girls."

"I might cry." Silence met the little girl's threat.

"You might cry harder when there's no cookies," he grunted. "Don't you attempt to blackmail me, you little swindler." Cassie giggled at his gruff tone. "I helped raise Merinus. You can't come up with a threat she didn't invent first. That woman was a terror on two legs. You can only hope to match her wiliness."

"I can do better, but I like you. Even if you did spank me. That's not daddy training, Kane." The little girl laughed. "Okay, four regular now. Two double later."

"Who said anything about later? Six a day limit, pup. You already had two. And if you sneak away from Dawn when she comes to collect you, I'll cut you off for sure. Spanking might not be daddy training, but discipline comes in somewhere, hotshot."

"Shew, you're tough as Momma. You sure you're not a daddy already, Kane?" The little girl's words splintered Sherra's heart.

"No, baby, I'm not a daddy." His soft, regretful tone destroyed her soul. "Come on, cookie time before Merrie comes in. She'll tan both our hides if we're not careful."

"I love you, Kane." The little girl sighed. "But if I don't talk to my momma soon, you're not going to have enough chocolate to bribe me with. Little girls need their mommas."

"Yes, baby, they do," he agreed softly. "More than anything, little girls need their mommas."

Sherra lowered her head, her hand clamping over her mouth as she turned and hurried quickly to the back of the house and into the late morning air. Tears tightened her chest, clogged her throat. A knife stroke of agony ripped through her soul as her womb pulsed in grief.

If you can't protect someone else's child how can you hope to protect your own? His furious words after Cassie's near-death still had the power to slice through her soul. He was right. She should have been ready for whatever Cassie would pull. They all knew how adept her hearing was. She should have thought, should have caught the little girl before she rushed through the door.

He had been furious, as terrified as she was when Cassie slipped away from her. Sherra knew he hadn't meant the words to be as hurtful as they had been, or the memories to rise inside her as bleak and black and they had.

Their child. She stopped in the shadow of one of the old oaks, her hands pressing her flat abdomen as her womb convulsed in need. The heat was building again. She couldn't conceive, would never conceive because of her own foolishness. Was it fate's sneering payment for having not protected the child she had carried the first time? She believed heavily in fate, in payment earned for any and all crimes against nature. Just as the world was now paying, as nature demanded the survival of the species science created, was fate exacting its own payment because she hadn't protected the life she had been given?

"Sherra, are you okay?" Callan's voice came through the communications unit she had clipped on before leaving her bedroom.

She drew in a deep breath. If he was watching the pinpoints on the monitors in the communications shed, he would know where she was and worry that she wasn't heading for the meeting he had arranged.

"I'm fine." She fought to keep her voice even, to keep her breathing calm. "I'm on my way in."

"We'll be waiting on you then," he responded quietly, though she knew she hadn't fooled him.

Damn, Doc probably told him about the test results, which would only make things worse. The increase in the hormone in her system was dramatic. Pretty soon, she would no longer to be able to fight, she'd be on her knees begging Kane to fuck her again.

The hormones in Kane's system, though increased, didn't seem to be affecting him as drastically as they were her. Even more worrisome was the strange tenderness around her womb, a slight swelling in the area of the fallopian tubes that had become more sensitive.

The heat was changing as well. The need was so much fiercer than it had ever been at this phase. She should have had two more weeks before entering the full phase of it, and even then, it hadn't been like this. This went beyond pain. Beyond hunger. It was a fire inside her that only Kane's release had quenched, and then, only for a while.

She drew in a hard breath and continued to the communications shed and the meeting Callan had called. The missile attack, followed so closely by Seth Lawrence's arrival, was worrying him as well as Kane. The information gained from the missile-wielding attacker had been anything but comforting. Learning that some unknown person or group was hiring assassins to get into the compound and kill Merinus, Roni and the child was frankly terrifying. It upped the stakes in an already dangerous game.

* * * * *

Kane flipped the lights back on and watched the expressions of the four people gathered in the makeshift office after the briefing on both the assassin who had struck days before and Aaron and Seth Lawrence.

The assassin was an irritation. An inept nobody who had found the caves that opened from the other side of the mountain and led into Breed territory. That would have to be taken care of. Aaron and Seth were a larger issue. The son, Kane was inclined to trust. The father was another matter entirely. His public stand on the Breeds was well-known, his opinion that they should be penned back up and kept closely guarded had been vocalized publicly several times.

"Double the guards in the forests," Callan said, his voice vibrating with an angry growl. "Have a unit start scouring the property for other caves, other entrances we're unaware of. Whoever strikes, they have to get past our perimeter security before they can strike the house. Let's make sure that doesn't happen again. Put extra guards on the guesthouse too. Make sure the Lawrence party stays put."

"Seth wouldn't hurt his sister." Dawn surprised them all when she spoke up then.

Her voice was firm, carrying an edge of steel that had slowly developed after Dayan's death. Her amber eyes regarded them all, the shadows of the past still swirling in the depths, though she no longer avoided their eyes.

"What makes you say that?" Kane asked her. His voice, though questioning, didn't outright reject her opinion either.

She pushed back the fringe of soft, light brown hair that fell over her forehead.

"I can't explain it." Dawn shook her head. "You can smell the truth just as easily as you can a lie," she told him, her voice low. "He's not lying, Kane."

"He's not the only one here, either," Kane reminded her. "What about the others?"

She seemed surprised that he asked her opinion.

"I don't know about the others," she finally said nervously. "Some people are easier to read."

He nodded quickly. "Okay, you shadow the son then, I'll put others on the father and chauffeur. Let me know what you sense, Dawn. We're all in this together. We combine our strengths and weaknesses. That's how we'll survive."

He was aware of Dawn's start of surprise, the slow confidence that built in her gaze as she watched him closely. But Sherra's look was like a physical caress. She was thrown off balance by the way he handled Dawn, but he didn't agree with the others and their intention to shelter her through any and all of life's hardships. She had been kicked too hard and too often in the past. Protecting her now would only harm the woman slowly emerging from her shell.

"That's it," Kane said decisively as they all rose to their feet. His gaze narrowed on his mate. "Except for you." He gave Sherra a mocking, sardonic smile despite the growing arousal tightening his body. "I still need to talk to you."

She lifted a brow. He hadn't spoken to her since the night before but he had noticed her nervousness and irritability as the meeting progressed. She was so damned hot she was nearly blazing.

He watched her now, his gaze touching on her swollen breasts, her nipples poking against the dark cloth of her uniform tank top, the way her gaze, when it touched upon him, turned hungry. No hungrier than his, though, he was certain. He was starving for the taste of her. His own lust had only increased since taking her the night before, the need for the unique, dark taste of her kiss was making him crazy.

"Don't fight with her, Kane," Callan grumped as he moved to the door with the others. "We're having a hard enough time getting along with her."

Sherra clenched her teeth as she stared back at her Pride leader.

"That is not true," she snapped.

Callan snorted. "Tell it to someone who doesn't have the scars from sparring with you, little sister. They might believe it."

A small warning growl was her only response as Callan chuckled and left the room, leaving Kane alone with her. He had watched the byplay between brother and sister, seeing the affection, the familial bond between them. Just as he shared one with Merinus.

"What do you want?" Sherra was damned irritable, he thought, just as Callan had warned. He also knew that irritability was one of the signs that accompanied her growing heat.

"Now there's a loaded question." Kane smiled slowly as he considered her. "Do you want a written list or do you have time for a verbal one? I could get rather descriptive verbally."

She flushed. A wash of gentle pink flushed her face as she crossed her arms over her obviously sensitive breasts and watched him warily. She was equal parts innocence and seductress. It drove him crazy, seeing the fluid sensuality in each movement, yet the complete innocence of just how damned sexy she was as she watched with such wary surprise.

He had fucked her the night before until she came, screaming into the cushions of the couch as her tight pussy clamped on his raging cock. He hadn't kissed her. He hadn't tasted the liquid heat that ran from between her thighs and now he was starving for it. He wouldn't wait much longer.

"Don't need a descriptive list, huh?" Kane asked regretfully as she continued to watch him with a flare of anger. "Fine. My main complaint is your nocturnal habits, which so far haven't been a problem. But I need you to start sticking closer to the house at night instead of venturing into the mountain."

"Why?" Sherra shifted restlessly.

Kane could see the refusal growing in her wary green eyes, the need for escape that was building in her body. He couldn't allow it. He had nearly had a stroke knowing she was facing that bastard with the missile launcher. According to Merinus, Callan was more than worried about the progress of the heat, concerned it would lessen her wariness, her ability to track and fight efficiently.

"That should be pretty obvious," he grunted as he moved closer to her. "If there are problems, I need you here to evacuate Merinus, Roni and Cassie. Besides that, we need to make certain the main Pride stays intact no matter what. That means you too, sweet pea."

Sherra winced at the nickname. "Kane, can the bullshit," she snapped, causing him to watch her with amused surprise. "You want me here for your convenience, nothing more. You keep hoping if I'm close enough that your round-the-clock fuck session will be harder for me to deny."

He was praying she would. He wondered if he should explain the difference between a hope and a prayer to her. Then decided perhaps it best, considering the slow rise of anger in her expression, that he hold off there.

He tilted his head, watching her curiously. "Well, there is that consideration, mate," he drawled instead.

She glared at him, her eyes glittering with suppressed anger and heated arousal.

"God, would you just let up," she muttered, surprising him with the quick about-face in her anger. "You act as though there hasn't been another woman for you in all these years while I should just bend over and give it up as though it were your due."

Kane sensed the underlying anger there. She was torn between what she knew was the truth and what she wanted to be the truth. His Sherra needed to hate, because loving hurt, but by God she wasn't the only one who had hurt through the years.

"There have been others," he finally acknowledged, hating it, hating the pain that flashed in her eyes. "It never happened easily, and never comfortably, but it happened."

He shook his head, remembering the few women he had touched, those he had fucked while he dreamed of Sherra, while he forced himself to ignore the distaste for the few moments of ease.

"There was no one else for me," she finally whispered, breaking his heart with the rough sound of her voice.

"And there is where you're wrong!" he snapped, refusing to allow the guilt he carried to weigh heavier upon his shoulders. "I thought you were dead. Gone, Sherra. Forever. You knew I was alive, you knew where to find me and you didn't. I won't regret the fact that there were nights I couldn't face alone. That there were memories that ate into my soul like a disease. I won't feel guilty for believing what you allowed me to believe, and I'll be damned if I'll let you hide from it. You were my fucking woman, and because of some quirk of nature, my mate. You hid. I didn't."

She swallowed tightly, her eyes dark, ravaged by the battles he could see waging within her soul. "It was one fucking kiss. There were no swollen glands, nothing…"

Kane smiled tightly. "One was all it took. Don't deny you're hotter than ever. I bet your pussy is so damned wet I could drown in it when I get my mouth down there. Just as it was then. The taste of spice and a spring rain. Your taste has haunted me, Sherra. All these years, endless nights that the craving for you nearly drove me insane."

Her face flamed, her eyes sparking with the fires raging inside her.

"Stop." She drew in a hard, deep breath as she backed away from him.

"Stop running from me, Sherra," he whispered softly as his arm hooked around her waist, pulling her to him. "I won't let you do that anymore. There's no reason to run."

"Look." She pressed her hands against his chest as though to push him away. "I told you last night, I can't risk this. Neither of us can. We don't know what will happen, Kane."

"I don't care what will happen, Sherra." And that was the end of the line as far as he was concerned. "Aren't you tired of hurting? Of aching? We could still the heat, baby."

He lowered his head, nuzzling at her ear, letting his lips whisper over the small shell as she shivered in response. Her fingers curled against his chest, her nails kneading it through the thin material of his shirt almost unconsciously.

"We could both regret it far too much later." Her voice was a hot little feminine sigh of need. "I can't just jump into this, Kane."

"Honey, I sucked every sweet drop of that drug out of your tongue yesterday and fucked you last night until you exploded around me," he told her harshly, his hands running down her back, over the flare of her buttocks as he allowed his fingers to clench into the smooth curves there. "If that wasn't jumping into it, then what is? Kiss me, Sherra. Don't keep punishing us both like this."

She was breathing just as hard and fast as he was when he raised his head enough to stare down at her. Her eyes were dazed, heavy-lidded, her soft pink lips parted and glistening with moisture. He licked his own lips, dying to taste her, to do the one thing that would make her so wild it would burn them both alive.

Her gaze centered on his lips, growing slumberous, her face softening with passion as she stared at them.

"I could eat you alive," he told her gently. "From your lips to your pussy, suck every sweet drop of moisture from them then get you hot and wet all over again before I slide my cock so deep inside you that you can't ever imagine refusing me again."

The thought of it, the need for it, had his body on fire, not to mention what it was doing to the erection throbbing in agony between his thighs. And she was thinking about it. He could see the lust pouring into her eyes, softening her against him as a whimper escaped her throat.

Sherra stared into the heated depths of Kane's eyes, seeing the determination, the lust raging through his body. His expression was tight, the flesh drawn over his cheekbones, his eyes narrowed, his lips heavy with sensuality. He was hard and he was horny and she had a feeling he was getting ready to drastically change the rules of the game they were playing.

"This is the wrong place for this." She pushed against his shoulders.

If she could just put some distance between them then maybe she could fight against the effects of the heat for at least one more day. One day could possibly turn into two, two into longer. The hormonal fires raging in her body never lasted longer than a month; she was already two weeks into it. If she could just hold him off a little longer.

"It's the perfect place for it."

He released her, but before she could gain her freedom he was at the strong steel door, locking it carefully before he turned back to her, his fingers going to the buttons of his shirt.

"Dammit, Kane!" she snapped. "Couches are not comfortable for fucking. Wait until we can find a bed."

"Then come to me while I'm around a bed," he told her, his voice clipped and impatient. "Now take those clothes off, Sherra, or you'll be wearing my shirt and nothing more when we leave, because I'll rip them off you."

Sizzling awareness surged through her body, even her toes tingled with the demanding tone in his voice.

"Get a grip," she hissed. "I am not going to let you fuck me here. Everyone will know what we did when we leave."

"Then *you* can fuck *me*," he growled, advancing on her. "But you're not leaving here until I've shot every damned drop of seed tormenting my cock up your pussy. So get naked, baby, because my control is on a very short leash right now."

Lust sucker-punched her womb. It had to be the heat that caused such a reaction. If he had said something so asinine any other time she would have kicked him. After clawing his eyes out. But now, her legs weakened and her breath caught at the sexual demand and she felt as stable as a weak noodle as she moved around the room, trying to maintain a reasonable distance.

"You've lost your mind." She tried to snarl, to inject some anger into her voice, but it came out breathless and panting instead.

If she could just get to the door.

He dropped his shirt from his shoulders. Strong, wide shoulders. Shoulders that flexed with strength and glistened with health. He was an aroused, determined male in his prime and he had made up his mind to fuck. Her pussy ached at the thought. The strength of the needy contractions flexing within her vagina warned her that she might not fight this as hard as she needed to.

"I've lost my patience," he corrected her, his eyes darkening as he somehow managed to maneuver her closer to the couch than she wanted to be. "I'm going to get you all naked, Sherra, and once I get my hands on you we both know it won't take long. After I rip those pants from your long pretty legs then I'm going to bury my mouth so deep in your wet cunt that there won't be an inch of it that doesn't know my touch."

She shivered. Shivered? Hell, she was shuddering, on the verge of climax from the force of his words alone.

"Kane." She tried to slip around him before he could stop her. It was as though he knew what she was going to do before she did. "This is insane. We'll never control this with you acting this way."

"Who says I want to control it?" he asked her devilishly. "No, baby. No control. No thinking. No excuses. Just you and me as hot as lava and burning down the world around us. Now, are you going to strip or do I strip you?"

He toed off the leather sneakers he had worn to the meeting. It was then she knew he had arranged this ahead of time. Kane never, ever wore sneakers around the compound. He wore the tough leather boots that protected his feet and lower legs while working.

She would have snapped something hateful at him then if his hands hadn't gone to his belt, the leather sliding free of the buckle as his fingers jerked the first button from his jeans loose.

"Damn you, my cock is on fire." He was nearly snarling as he released the button of his jeans. "And you're still dressed, Sherra. Don't make me tear those clothes off you."

Sherra swallowed tightly as his jeans and briefs were kicked free of his hard body. His cock strained toward her, heavy and engorged, the plum-shaped, purplish head beaded with pre-come and looking too tempting for her comfort.

"Kane," she whispered, barely managing not to whimper in need. "This is not a good idea."

"Best idea I've had in eleven years," he informed her, his voice harsh as he moved too fast for her to evade.

Before she could run, before she could even consider fighting, he had her on her back on the wide couch, his hands at the bottom of her stretchy top as he jerked it over her breasts.

"Hell, yeah," he muttered, his hands enclosing her breasts as his lips lowered to hers.

She could have fought him, she assured herself. She could have pushed away, fought her way to the door, she could have escaped. A lie to salve her pride? Did it matter, she wondered? Because a second later his lips covered hers and escape was the last thing on her mind.

He didn't give her a chance to fight him, but Sherra knew she should have never expected him to. His lips slanted over hers, his tongue plunging past her lips as she gasped, twining immediately with hers.

His tongue was cool, soothing against hers as the caress began to rub against the swollen glands, allowing the hormone contained there its freedom. Sherra had thought it would be enough, that the small relief would give her a chance to regain her control. It was the opposite of that. Everything inside her clenched and flamed in yearning. She needed more. She needed him sucking the hormone from her, drawing it into himself. The powerful demands of nature were more than she could deny.

Her arms wrapped around his shoulders, her hands spearing into his hair as she fought for dominance in at least this one thing. Her tongue battled and twined as mewling whimpers escaped her throat until he allowed her to slide her tongue past his waiting lips.

The first draw of his mouth on the swollen extension had her body bowing tight. Sensation tore through her, a pleasure so overwhelming it knotted her womb with a convulsive shudder of agonized hunger. Her breasts were so sensitive that each stroke of his fingers over her nipples caused a helpless scream to echo past her lips, so desperate for the stroke of his cock up her pussy that she was pushing at her pants, fighting to free herself of them so he could plunge inside her.

Their tongues twined within his mouth as his lips sucked at the spicy fluid that came from the mating glands. It soothed the sensitivity, the heat that seemed to fill her own tongue, but only increased the heat throughout her body.

She was mindless, so greedy, so hungry for him now that nothing mattered except the hard thrust she knew was coming.

"Not yet." The growl that tore from his throat as he pulled back from her lips was rough, guttural. "First...what I've dreamed of, Sherra."

He ripped the top from her a second before he moved to her pants. He got them to her ankles before he realized he was going to have to unlace her boots and remove them first.

"Fuck it," he snarled.

Placing his hands at her knees, he raised them, then spread her wide as he lowered his mouth to the swollen, wet curves of her aching cunt.

His tongue circled her clit with a ring of exquisite fire as he hummed in appreciation.

"You're so damned wet I could drown in you," he growled before licking again.

It was a firm, destructive caress that went around and around her engorged clit, the sensations making her hips writhe as he stoked the fire in her pussy higher, hotter.

"Kane, I can't stand it," she panted, her hands clenching into the cushions of the couch as she fought to keep her sanity. "Please, don't torture me like this."

A rough laugh vibrated against her wet flesh. "Torture you?" he asked gutturally. "Sherra, baby, you don't understand, if I don't taste you I'm going to go out of my mind. All I can think of is the taste of your kiss, your hot little pussy. How you screamed for me, how you came in my mouth. Come for me, baby, fill the hunger and then I'll fulfill yours."

She screamed his name as his tongue swiped through the bare slit of her cunt, a slow, appreciative lick as he hummed in pleasure.

"Fuck. Addictive," he groaned. "I've never forgotten, Sherra, your sweet taste, your heat. I'll die needing you..."

Sherra's head thrashed against the couch as she cried out in rising demand. Her body was stretched, taut, every cell tightening with the rapid arcs of pleasure whipping through her.

She fought to get closer, to grind her aching flesh into his mouth. The near urgency, the need for release, the clenching, brutal spasms of need flexing her womb were killing her. Her clit was a swollen knot of burning need, her vagina an ever-tightening cauldron of lust.

"Kane. God. I can't stand it..." Her legs were trapped by her own clothing, her knees held wide by his hands as he devoured the thick syrup of her response, drawing it into his mouth, licking and groaning against her, delving into the blistering depths of her pussy for more.

"Kane, please." She nearly screamed his name. She couldn't bear the pitiless convulsions in her womb any longer. Her body was in demand and only one thing would or could ease it. "Please. Please, Kane. Fuck me. I'm begging you..."

He groaned helplessly, his tongue plunging deep and hard inside her vagina, fucking her into a mindless frenzied urgency. She had never known anything so hot, or a hunger so deep.

His tongue stoked the fires hotter, eating at her, lapping at her, until tremors of sensation shook her body remorselessly.

"I can't get enough of you," he groaned as he dragged his head from her pulsing cunt. "I'm starved for you, Sherra."

He rose to his knees, his cock heavy and engorged as he reached for her, forcing her to turn as she gasped in surprise. He pulled at the ties of one boot, removed it and then slid her pants leg off as he moved between her thighs.

There were few preliminaries. The need was too explosive, she had forced them to wait too long and Kane was hungry. His cock plunged inside her, forcing its way past fist-tight muscles, stretching her with brutal strokes as his back arched, his hips working furiously as he fought to hold back the building climax.

Sherra couldn't restrain her scream of pleasure or her own writhing hips. She worked her cunt on the thick cock pistoning in and out of her vagina. Her legs clasped his hips, her back arched, and within minutes she dissolved. Hard, racking, the shudders of orgasm tightened her body to near breaking point as pleasure ripped through her. Not just pleasure...ecstasy, rapture, a blinding sensitivity she would have never believed possible if she hadn't experienced it herself. It was almost never-ending, contraction after contraction tightening around his thrusting erection until it trapped him deep inside her, milking every drop of thick creamy seed trapped inside his balls.

His hands were hard on her hips, his male cries harsh and pulled roughly from the depths of his chest as his body shook above her for long seconds. Finally, blissfully, the violent tremors of rapturous pleasure eased, releasing him to clasp against her, his mouth at her neck as he fought for breath. And he was still hard.

Sherra blinked back tears of weary knowledge. The Breed males were exceptionally powerful, built for endurance, allowing them to hold up beneath the intense eroticism of the mating heat. How would Kane endure it?

"I'm going to fuck you until neither of us can move," he whispered at her neck as he began to thrust inside her again. "Until there's nothing left of you or me, Sherra. Only us. Only the knowledge that you'll never..." a hard thrust lifted her to him with a weak cry of growing hunger, "ever..." deeper, harder, "fucking refuse me again..."

Chapter Nine

Kane helped her dress and carried her to his room hours later. Sherra was limp, exhausted in his arms and his cock was still hard, raging with the need to be buried inside her again. As he undressed her and tucked her in the bed he sat down heavily in the chair beside it after undressing himself and just stared at her.

She was sleeping deeply — so deeply that the move had barely disturbed her. Dark shadows lay under her eyes, a testament to the sleepless nights she had spent over the last few weeks. Nights spent pacing her room or roaming the mountain. Just as he had spent his nights.

He leaned his head wearily against the back of the chair and closed his eyes. His erection throbbed like a damned toothache. He couldn't get enough of her. Couldn't spill his seed inside her fast enough or hard enough for satisfaction.

He smiled slowly. It would kill him, but damn if she wasn't worth it. She was tight and hot, fitting him perfectly, gripping his cock like a silken glove and making him work to fit the entire length inside her. No matter how slick and wet she got she was fist-tight around his bursting erection.

Not that he was overly large, but he wasn't lacking either.

He watched her, his heart heavy now, his emotions as jumbled together as his desires were.

God alone knew how much he loved her. Loved her until his heart had ripped from his chest when he thought she was dead. He hadn't wanted to live, hadn't wanted to go on, it had hurt so bad to be without her. Every cell of his body had mourned her for eleven long, empty years.

The night she had stepped from the shadows in Sandy Hook he had breathed for the first time since losing her. His heart had begun beating again, blood refreshing his body, reminding him he was indeed alive after that long emotional hibernation he had gone into. Suddenly, nothing else had mattered but touching her, holding her. Being a part of her. And she had hated him. He had seen it in her eyes, a pain that darkened the soul, a fury he could never extinguish by himself.

He grimaced at the reasons behind it. Surging to his feet he pulled a pair of loose jogging pants on, wincing as his cock tented the fabric away from his body.

Pacing to the balcony doors he stared into the darkness silently.

She had lost their child, been raped, had suffered through a reaction to the drugs the scientists had given her with such violence it had nearly killed her. And even after the escape her torment hadn't been over. She had endured years of building arousal so intense the physical pain was destructive. She had suffered in ways he could never imagine, and sometimes he wondered if it would ever end.

Kane crossed his arms over his chest as he sighed wearily. He had forced her into accepting the mating heat. Had taken her kiss, knowing she would have no choice after the hormone was shared between them. Was he any better than the guards who had raped her in those labs?

"Kane." He turned quickly to her voice.

She lay watching him, her green eyes darkening as she glimpsed his aroused body.

"You're hurting," she said softly, moving to pull the blankets back from her naked body.

"No." He was there before she could finish the move. "You should sleep, baby. You're exhausted."

She frowned in confusion. "You're aroused, Kane."

"I've been aroused for the last eleven years." He grinned wryly. "A few more hours won't hurt me."

Her gaze flickered with emotion before it was quickly shielded by the thick, white- blonde lashes he so loved.

"What if it doesn't go away for you?" she asked him. "How can you bear it, Kane?"

Shaking his head he moved beside her, propping his shoulders against the headboard as he pulled her against his chest. She resisted for a second before sprawling over him as he wanted. Almost boneless, like the lazy little cat she should be, he thought with a grin. It wouldn't bother him if she was draped across him twenty-four hours a day, seven days a week.

"Sherra, I've been like this since before our first kiss. I have a lot of time to make up for. It will be quite a while before we've slaked the hunger that's built up over the years," he told her with a thread of amusement. "Don't you worry about me. Worry about you for now. I don't want you hurting anymore. I can't stand to see the arousal and the need shadowing your eyes when there's nothing I want more than to ease it however I can."

He kissed the top of her head, male pride filling his chest at the tangled condition of her hair. His fingers had messed it up, had torn it from the neat braid she normally kept it in. Her body was sexily boneless, warm and satiny against his flesh. His balls tightened with the need to make her scream his name again.

She was silent for long moments, thinking. That worried him. Sherra never failed to piss him off when she started thinking. The woman's mind was like a steel trap, sharp and always effective as hell. But she was a female and he'd be damned if he could make sense of a female's mind at the best of times. Maybe fucking her wasn't a bad idea. At least then she would stop thinking.

"I thought you left me," she finally said, her voice low, thick with emotion. "For so long, I thought you had just left. At first, it hurt, but I had the baby…" Her voice broke as his arms tightened around her.

Everything in Kane shattered again at the pain in her voice. He buried his head in her hair and fought the emotion ripping through him.

"I could have survived with our baby, Kane," she whispered. "I dreamed of a little boy that looked like you, that laughed like you." He could hear the regret, soul-deep, the dreams she had buried so far inside her. "I died in those labs, Kane. You can't resurrect something that no longer has life."

Kane shook his head, a whisper of a smile crossing his lips. Yep, female logic sucked, he thought, not for the first time. And this woman's was sure to drive him insane.

"Sherra, baby, I'm sure as hell you believe every word that just came out of your mouth," he finally said gently. "But that's the biggest crock of bull I ever heard in my life."

She stiffened and would have risen from his chest if he hadn't held her still.

"Stay right the hell where you are before I fill your mouth with my dick, so I don't have to listen to such nonsense," he warned her. "Dead, my ass. If you were dead, Sherra, you wouldn't ache. You wouldn't hurt. You wouldn't give a damn how hot and horny I got or whether or not that sizzling hormone you put out would hurt me. You would fuck the hell out of me, get off and be done with it."

He could feel the anger building in her. Better the anger than that damned certainty that there was no love left within her. He wouldn't accept that. He wouldn't let her accept that.

"You're such an asshole, Kane." She jerked back from him, her eyes glittering fury. "Do you have to think you're always right? You haven't survived these years with me…"

"I would have," he snarled back at her, amazed at how quickly his lust was beginning to build now. "I wasn't with you by your choice, Sherra. You decided not to let me know. You decided to let me believe you were dead. You decided, baby, so don't even attempt to discredit me because I wasn't with you."

"Oh yeah, I should have just called. 'Oh, hi, Kane baby, I lived through the fire but I miscarried our baby. Would you please come fuck me again even though I believe you lied and left me to begin with?'" she snapped sarcastically. "Not hardly, stud."

Stud. His cock jerked. He'd show her *stud*.

"That would have worked for me," he told her irritably, watching her carefully.

Her face was flushed, her eyes glittering dangerously. But he could see her arousal building, the perspiration that dampened her forehead, the state of her hard, baby pink nipples. His mouth watered to cover them, suck them, hear her scream as she begged for his cock.

"I just bet it would have." She slapped at him as he moved, pushing her to the bed, restraining her hands to the mattress as he straddled her. "Get off me, moron. Merinus is right—you're an asshole, plain and simple. You're not worth talking to."

"Then don't talk," he snapped furiously. "Because I'll be damned if you make sense when you do. Put that smart-assed mouth to some good use and kiss me instead."

Chapter Ten

Kiss him she did. Furious, hungry, desperate, their mouths mated, tongues twining, giving and taking until Sherra thought she would explode from the pleasure of that alone. He infuriated her. He drove her insane. But below it all was this need. This terrible physical and emotional hunger that she could never still.

Sherra was smart enough to know that it went beyond just the mating heat. There was a need that curled inside her very soul, stretched and roared in demand. She whimpered beneath the onslaught of heated yearning and awakening emotion, her body clenching, tightening, as her nails bit into Kane's hard shoulders and her tongue pressed passionately into his mouth.

His lips closed on it, his mouth drawing on the swollen flesh as he pushed her thighs apart his hands moved between her and the sweat pants he wore, quickly ridding himself of the offending material. His lips sipped at hers, his tongue stroking, fueling the lust building between them as he positioned his erection, sliding it between her plump pussy lips as he groaned roughly.

Sherra could feel the moisture there slickening the broad head of his cock, preparing her for the invasion that she knew would take her past all her preconceived notions of pleasure. There was nothing like being touched by Kane. Being held and loved by him.

"You're so hot," he whispered when he tore his lips from hers. "So hot and sweet, baby, it's like being surrounded by the sweetest fire on earth. Burn me again, Sherra."

His lips buried at her throat as he began to work his cock inside her. Short, fierce thrusts that opened her, stretched her, had her screaming for more of the erotic pain that built inside her cunt.

"There, kitty. So sweet and hot. You fit me perfectly," he groaned roughly as the last inches slid in, seating him fully inside her, sending impulses of exquisite pleasure ricocheting through her body. She could feel him, so thick and hard, wedged inside her, stretching her until the boundary between pleasure and pain could no longer be distinguished.

"Look at me, Sherra," he whispered, his voice strained as he raised his head, bracing his weight on his elbows as he stared down at her intently. "Look at me, baby. See how wild you make me. See me, Sherra. Just this once."

Her breath hitched at the huskily spoken plea. His eyes mesmerized her. So deep, dark and filled with emotion, haunted with pain and pleasure as he moved slowly inside the convulsive grip of her pussy. Her womb flexed as he stared down at her, the eroticism of watching his face flush, his eyes glitter with sexual hunger, filled her like a surge of electrical energy. Her hips jerked, driving him deeper as her neck arched, his hands tugging at her hair where they threaded snugly within the strands.

"Tell me it feels good, Sherra." A slow, sexy smile shaped his swollen lips as his cheeks flushed a deep, brick red. "Talk to me, darlin'. Let me hear your voice, sweet and low and rough from needing me."

"You're crazy," she gasped as his hips rotated, his cock screwing into her deeper when she thought it wasn't possible for him to get further inside her. "You want me to talk to you?"

"Mmm," he murmured, lowering his head just enough to kiss the corner of her lips before he rose again, watching her carefully. "Tell me how good my cock feels inside you, Sherra. Do you like this…?"

Her back arched, a low, fierce growl emitting from between her lips as he pulled back several inches then thrust in deep again. Nerve endings caught fire, her womb convulsed and a shiver of impending release shuddered through her body. She could feel it, just out of reach, despite the fact that he was doing little more than filling her sensitive pussy, his cock throbbing like another heartbeat inside her.

"Yes. Yes. I like that." She writhed beneath him, the pleasure whipping through her like an impending firestorm. "More."

"More?" His hands tugged at her hair as his hips rotated again, the head of his erection stroking her sensitive flesh, sending building waves of sensation tearing through her.

What was he doing to her? Why was he delaying the release she knew tormented him as well? Sherra could feel the building sensations bordering on pain within her own body. Each thrust sent her higher, closer, but they were too few to send her over the edge.

"More," she panted, her fingers digging into his shoulders. "What do you want, Kane? Do you want me to beg?"

He was driving her crazy. She fought to drive her cunt harder onto the impalement of his cock, but he used his weight to hold her to the bed, to control the movement of her hips as her legs rose to wrap around his lower back.

"I want what you gave me the first time, Sherra," he told her. "I know you haven't forgotten. You couldn't have forgotten." For a moment his voice was tortured, his expression flickering with pain as perspiration dampened his features.

Yes. She remembered. Every moment of that night, every touch, every…

She whispered a protest, her gaze going to his roughly scarred chest and the mark she had left so long ago.

She had whispered to him before placing the wound. Words that echoed in her mind, filled her with lust and left her longing for the same haunting need she glimpsed in his eyes.

"Kane." She protested the rising hunger to go back, to allow the dreams to take over once again.

"I'll never leave you again, Sherra." He stilled inside her as she stared up at him in shock.

Her soul wailed in misery at his words.

"Stop." She shook her head desperately. "Not now. Not yet."

She couldn't deal with the overload of emotions while his cock was straining the walls of her pussy, the need for orgasm beating at her brain.

"Now." He denied her the ability to hide any longer. And hiding, she knew, was exactly what she had been doing. "Here, now, Sherra."

His hips bunched as he began slowly—too damned slowly for the needs rocking through her—pumping inside her just enough to keep the pain from clawing at her womb, but not enough for orgasm.

"Do you like that, baby? Do you like feeling my cock fucking inside your tight pussy, making us both crazier by the second?" he asked her softly, an echo of the past. "Tell me what you want, Sherra. I'll give you anything you want."

"No." Her head thrashed against the mattress as she fought the potent, irresistible call of her own soul, and the needs hammering at her brain. "Stop this, Kane. Please. Just let me come."

"No," he growled, baring his teeth as his own body shuddered with the need. "Not yet. Feel it, baby. Feel how good it is."

He drove inside her hard, paused, his cock throbbing heavily inside the sensitive clasp of her pussy.

"Kane…" She sobbed his name.

"Now…" He drove inside her again. Paused. His eyes watched her, glittering wildly, hunger and demand tightening every line of his expression. "Now."

"Oh God." Her hips jerked at the next hard thrust, her head turning, her tongue swiping over the mark on his chest as he suddenly stilled. "Fuck me, Kane. Fuck me hard and hot until nothing matters but us. Nothing but us..." Her mouth covered the spot, her teeth raking over it, then her tongue, a second before she bit him.

A male shout of satisfaction filled the room as he began to move. One hand lowered to her hip as his own began to churn, thrust, driving his cock deep and hard inside her as she tasted blood. Her tongue, rasping and filled with the unique mating hormone, began to lap at the wound, her mouth sucking at his flesh as the taste of him became the final straw to drive her past reason. Her orgasm erupted, her pussy tightening on his driving cock as she tore her mouth from his chest to scream out her completion.

"Fuck yes. Come for me, baby." His head buried at her neck as he stroked inside her powerfully, lengthening, driving her orgasm higher until reality, past and present, was extinguished. There were only her and Kane. Together, melting, blending, orgasm and bonding clashed and in the fires of their release, satisfaction weaved for the first time in years, two hearts beat, bonded, and eased. For now, there was peace.

* * * * *

Seth Lawrence had seen many things in his life. At thirty-five, he guessed he would have experienced damned near every adventure a man of his temperament could have imagined. He had spoiled himself with the darker edge of life, but nothing had prepared him for Dawn Daniels. He had read her file. Age twenty-seven, Cougar Breed, the horrors recorded from the Lab files didn't bear thinking of. She had endured a hell no child should have ever lived.

Her golden-brown eyes were haunted with that past, deep, somber pools of suspicion and hunger. Not sexual hunger, but the soul-deep, mind-consuming hunger to live. He bet the sizeable fortune he possessed that Dawn had never known either a lover's touch or a friend's gentle embrace without remembering the fear and the nightmares of her past.

Now, she stood within the guesthouse of Sanctuary, watching him with those mysterious pools of emotion, her body stiff, defensive as she answered to his latest demands. He hid his smile, rubbing his finger over his lips as his elbow braced on the padded arm of the couch and his knee bent, his foot resting on the teak coffee table in front of him.

"You're not in a position to demand anything, Mr. Lawrence," she reminded him severally, the high cheekbones and kittenish angles of her face revealed by the severity of the French braid which pulled her hair back from her face. Soft, golden-brown strands, not nearly as dark as the color of her eyes, like rich, light caramel. "Sanctuary is not one of your offices," she continued. "My men are not under your command."

Her men? His brows snapped into a frown. He didn't like the way she phrased that. Her guards perhaps? Yeah, he could handle that phrase.

"Furthermore, may I also remind you that you are here only under objection. If it wasn't for Cassie, you'd be recuperating in a hospital rather than reclining on that damned couch staring at me as though I were a bug under a microscope."

His brow lifted. Actually, he was watching her like the tempting little package she was. Her short, compact little body was driving him crazy. Tempting breasts pressed against the soft cotton of her dull green T-shirt and that gun strapped to her thigh, over the snug mission pants she wore, should not have been sexy. He was more a pervert than he believed, because his cock was spike-hard as she faced him so defiantly.

"I believe the phrase 'watching you like a tender morsel of meat' would be more appropriate." He held back his smile just as he tried to dim the interest in her response in his gaze.

She jerked alert, her jaw tightening, her lightly tanned face paling the barest bit as her gaze darkened. Then she snarled.

His cock jerked, flexing in a harsh reminder of its aroused state as she flashed those pearly canines.

"Don't make the mistake of thinking you can play with me, Lawrence," she growled, but he saw her nipples harden, caught the quick intake of her breath. "I could tear you apart before you knew what hit you."

He smiled then. A slow, confident curve of his lips as his gaze went over her once again.

"Play with you?" he murmured softly. "I'd actually be quite serious, darling, never doubt that for a moment."

Had he had ever wanted a woman as swiftly, as heatedly as he did this one? It wasn't possible. He would remember a hunger this strong, this consuming. As he continued to watch her, her face flushed, paled, then flushed again. Her breathing became harder, faster. But her hand dropped to her gun, her fingers caressing the handgrip as though seeking reassurance.

"Don't make that mistake, Lawrence." Her voice chilled, but catching the undercurrent of pain, of anger, wasn't hard. "Better men than you have tried. They failed."

"They weren't men." He didn't move, despite the need to jerk to his feet, to pace in fury, to pull her to him and fill his senses with the taste of her. "Rabid animals, Dawn, don't count."

Her hand tightened on the gun as regret filled her eyes.

"Don't fool yourself into thinking I'll fall at your feet as the women who fill your life do," she snapped, her shoulders straightening, which only pressed her breasts tighter against her shirt, her nipples clearly revealed beneath it. Hard, pointed tips he would give his left nut to taste. Well, maybe not a nut, but damned near anything else.

"I'd be disappointed if you did, sweetheart." He braced his arm over his upraised knee as he fought to maintain a relaxed, calm demeanor. Now wasn't the time to spook her. He wanted her off balance, not running from him. "I'm merely stating the obvious. You said I was watching you like a bug under a microscope. I'm actually watching you like the very beautiful woman you are, nothing more."

"I'm an animal. One it would pay you to be wary of," she snarled, flashing those wickedly sharp teeth again.

Son of a bitch cock, it flexed painfully, more interested than it should have been.

His eyes went over her again.

"You guys have a thing about being animals, don't you?" he stated then. "I've heard that comment several times this week. If that's what you truly believe, then why the hell are you trying to mix with the rest of us? Where's the closest pen, Dawn, I'll help you lock yourself in."

He was pushing, he knew was, and he couldn't help it. It infuriated him to hear her describe herself in such a way, to see the belief flashing in her eyes. It enraged him to remember how the belief had been beaten into her. As a child, nothing more, raped by Council soldiers, jeered at, forced to be the animal they called her.

"I can kill you and get away with it." Her voice was hoarse now. "And I wouldn't regret it. I'll sleep just as well as I do every other night…"

"You don't sleep, period," he retorted, his anger finally showing as she faced him, her expression drawn with exhaustion, nightmares haunting her eyes. And he couldn't even explain why he fucking cared. "A child could see how little sleep you get, woman. Pull the badass Breed persona on me, it doesn't work. You could kill me in a heartbeat but you'd never forget it." He leaned forward then, watching her, knowing she would run, just as he knew he'd never let her go. "You would never forget, Dawn, that you killed the one man capable of holding you during the nightmares, of accepting who you are, and all that entails."

"So you think you can cure the nightmares?" She sneered then. "Letting you touch me would just wipe it all away, huh, Seth?"

"No," he whispered, watching her pale again, but this time, the color didn't return. "Nothing can wipe it away, Dawn.

Nothing can change the past or the nightmares. But I would be there when you awoke. You wouldn't be alone anymore, and in time, maybe, better dreams could take their place sometimes."

She stepped back, retreating as a nerve jerked at the corner of her lip an instant before the animalistic snarl sounded from her throat.

"Touch me and you'll die."

Her hand gripped the gun, her fingers closing over the butt with a desperation he could feel inside himself.

"Even if you ask me?" he questioned her, keeping his voice gentle, calm, when he wanted to rage at the pain in her eyes.

"I'll never ask you, Seth," she bit out painfully, staring back at him with eyes that haunted his darkest dreams. "I'll never ask, whether I want it or not, no matter the circumstances. Ever. Do you understand me? I'll never lie beneath you, you're fooling yourself…"

"So lie above me."

She flinched, her eyes widening as she swallowed with a tight, convulsive movement.

"One of the others will be by later to discuss seeing your sister. I have work to do."

"Dawn." He came to his feet as she turned away, expecting what would happen, his expression never changing as she spun back, the gun slipping expertly from the holster, pointing to the center of his chest as she gripped it with both hands, her finger on the trigger.

He stared at the weapon for a long moment before he raised his eyes to hers, seeing the tears swimming within them, the agony reflected there.

"Aren't you tired of being alone? I am." He made no other move, just stared back at her, his chest tight with emotions he wasn't certain he was comfortable with, needs he knew she could never accept.

"Stay away from me." Her voice was strong, brooking no refusal, grating with purpose and determination. "Stay away, Seth, or we'll both regret it."

She holstered the weapon, turned and almost ran from the house. He heard the front door slam, felt her absence in a way he couldn't explain, even to himself. Regret filled him, slammed through him.

"Bad mistake, man, letting her see it." Taber stepped from the kitchen, as soundless as the animal whose DNA he carried as he stepped into the living room.

"Did I ask for your advice?" Rage was eating him. His temper was a precarious thing right now, he'd be damned if he would force himself to deal.

"You didn't have to ask," the other man growled. "Not that I expect you to listen to me. Kane didn't. But if you're serious, soul serious about her, don't let her know it. Don't let her see it. Don't let her suspect it. She'll run herself to the ground fighting it if you do."

"And I'll be there to pick her up." He turned to Taber, uncertain how to handle the emotions raging in him now. What Dawn made him feel, terrified him sometimes.

"If there's anything left to pick up," Taber pointed out, his voice soft, regretful. "That's your greatest battle, man. Making sure there's something left to love, rather than bury."

Chapter Eleven

Peace didn't last for long for Kane. He feigned sleep the next morning as Sherra slipped from his bed and sneaked as silent as a thief from the bedroom. As the door closed, he opened his eyes and sighed wearily as he stared up at the ceiling. Breaking through the woman's reserve was going to be the death of him.

Lifting his hand, he scratched at his chest absently, the light itch around the mating mark Sherra had left years before another reminder of his tie to her. Not that being tied to her bothered him, fact was, he loved her more than he loved his own life. There were few things that meant more to him than that blonde-haired little hellcat did. Hell, he didn't think anything mattered more than she did. Getting her to admit she felt the same was going to be the damned death of him. If this fucking erection didn't beat her to it.

He cast a resigned, half-irritated, half-amused look toward his lap where the sheet tented over his hard dick.

Shaking his head and giving a half growl, he rose from the bed and headed for the shower. He considered a cold shower, but had learned the hard way that it didn't help in the least. Besides, every bone and muscle in his body ached from the exhaustion slowly taking over. The lack of sleep, the worry, the damned arousal were combining to kill him. Sherra wouldn't have to worry much longer about his harassing her, he thought as he stepped beneath the hard pounding spray of the shower. He was going to die from a fucking hard-on.

Work. It had filled in the missing places in his life for years now, it would serve him a while longer. The Breed sanctuary still suffered from security weaknesses and fools' attacks. Not to mention those damned Lawrence aggravations they were trying to hide in one of the compound's houses. Shit was starting to get real deep here, and he was getting fucking sick of avoiding the various piles everyone was trying to hide.

After dressing, he clipped his holstered weapon to his belt and left his room, mentally going over a very long list of various duties awaiting his attention. Communications upgrades, intel from various sources left through the night, security protocols and logs from the past twelve hours from individual patrol leaders. It went on and on, dragging at his shoulders as he neared the top of the stairs.

"How dare you hide this from me?" Roni's voice met Kane as he came downstairs. The tension in the compound was getting to them all. The enforced confinement was driving Merinus and Roni crazy and in turn they were driving them all crazy. He crossed his arms over his chest and watched curiously as Roni gave her mate hell.

There wasn't much that he gained more pleasure from than watching the irritable, irritating Jaguar Breed get what-for, from his ever-loving mate.

The dark-haired beauty faced Taber, her fists clenched at her sides, tears streaking down her face as she screamed at him. Taber was pale, his eyes desperate as he stared at his wife.

This didn't look good. Kicking his ass over some perceived slight never made Roni mad enough cry. This wasn't a hormonal ass-chewing. Which wasn't good.

"Roni, you don't understand." Taber ran his hands over his face in irritation. "I was going to tell you. As soon as I thought you were strong enough…"

Uh-oh. It appeared shit had hit the fan here, and Roni was well aware of the hidden guests gracing the estate.

"You fuck me until I can't breathe but you think I'm not strong enough to talk?"

Kane winced. Boy, did she have him there.

"The situation is too dangerous…"

"And you're too full of shit." Her finger poked into his chest. "They're my family. All I have left. After the hell my stepfather put me through I can't believe you would hide this from me."

"That was why, dammit," Taber cursed. "Roni, please, you have to understand…"

"I don't have to do jack," she snapped. "You, on the other hand, better find another bed."

Taber, without his mate to help rid him of some of that excess energy that fueled his temper? Kane didn't think so.

"A Feline divorce," Kane quipped as he came down the stairs. "Can I watch? I might need to take notes."

Taber snarled as they turned to face him, canines flashing, green eyes glowing with rage as he found a target to hate. Roni's eyes flashed with fury.

"Did I ask for your help?" she asked Kane angrily.

Kane shrugged. "You don't have to ask, Roni. I told you, I'll give you and Merinus advice for free. It's the least I can do, seeing as how you're chained to such rude, deceptive beings as these Felines." He smiled with all the male innocence he could muster. It wasn't much, but it was enough to heat an already hot situation.

"I'm going to rip your fucking throat out, Tyler," Taber promised him.

Kane lifted a brow mockingly. "Hey, it's not my fault you thought you knew what she could handle. She's an adult. Hell, let her live for a change."

Taber's snarl was violent.

"This is none of your business," Roni informed him snidely. "Go away, Kane."

He glanced at Taber and shrugged. "See? She's perfectly capable of handling betrayal. You worried too much."

"He did not betray me," Roni gasped, turning on him now. "What is your damned problem?"

Kane shrugged. "He's an ill-tempered bag of misfit genetics who lied to you. You deserve better."

"He didn't lie," she snapped.

Taber was growling like the rabid panther he was. Kane loved it. The other man's hands were effectively tied for the moment as long as pleasing his mate meant more than his fury.

"He didn't?" Kane frowned. "Then why are you so pissed?"

"Because he didn't tell me, asshole." Her snarl rivaled Taber's.

Kane gave Taber a disapproving glance. "Shame on you." He turned back to Roni. "You're splitting hairs. Deception is deception. I know a good divorce lawyer. I could get his number for you."

Her mouth opened then snapped closed as she growled at him with a baring of teeth that made him more than a little nervous. Taber should be taking lessons from her.

"Do you think I don't know what you're up to, buster?" she asked him furiously. "If you want a fight with Taber so damned bad then here he is. Fight with him alone. I'm sure he'll bring me *your* skin before the day is over because you're a moron. I don't want to divorce him, all I wanted to do was yell at him for being so damned arrogant and you just had to fucking ruin it."

She stomped out of the room as her mate stared at her incredulously then turned back to Kane.

"I can't believe she is giving me permission to kick your arrogant ass now." Taber shook his head wearily. "I have a feeling I should be thanking you, but I haven't figured out what for yet."

Kane chuckled. "Hell, if she was really mad, she would have shot you. Go take her to meet her daddy and then pet her when she's crying over it and she'll be okay. Pregnancy hormones are a bitch." He grinned. "Merinus is driving Callan crazy with them."

Kane moved for the front door when a hand on his shoulder stopped him. He turned back, watching as Taber shifted uncomfortably.

"I don't like seeing Sherra hurting," Taber finally said in frustration. "And I sure as hell don't like the little insults you seem to throw out so easily, but thanks. I was afraid she was ready to walk out for good."

"No problem, cat boy. Just don't start purring all over me or I might have to shoot you myself." He shrugged his shoulders, not in the least comfortable with Taber's sudden shift in mood.

Taber laughed mockingly as he shook his head at Kane's response.

"Callan's right," he said. "You really can't help yourself. You know someone will kill you for those insults eventually, don't you?"

"Yeah, yeah," Kane snorted. "I expect to hear your celebration clear into the deepest depths of hell. Now I have work to do even if you don't. Later, purr bag."

* * * * *

"You're in trouble there, Sis." Sherra flinched as Taber's voice echoed up the stairs after Kane's departure. "I have to admit, he kind of grows on you."

She had watched the confrontation herself, amazed at how easily Kane had managed to diffuse Roni's anger. But she had seen something else, too. She had seen the way his shoulders tensed, the flash of concern on his expression as his profile turned to her. He cared.

She shook her head, realizing then how much Kane did care about them all. It wasn't the first time he had drawn someone's anger to him rather than allow it to grow into an explosive situation between others. His shoulders were broad and strong, but she wondered how much longer he could shoulder the burdens he often took on.

"Yeah, I realize that." Sherra walked down the stairs, tugging on her black jacket and adjusting the comm link to her ear as she headed for the front door. "I've known that for a long time now, Taber."

She had been in trouble from the first day he showed up in her life at those damned labs.

Taber shook his head as he approached her, his green eyes darker than her own and much too perceptive. He drew in a deep breath, a frown crossing his brow.

"Have you been in to see Doc yet?" he asked her.

Sherra shook her head. "Not yet. I called this morning and told him I would be in later, why?"

Taber shook his head, his brow creasing into a frown. "I'm not sure, but make certain you don't miss that appointment. Your scent has altered in some way, I just can't put my finger on how."

Sherra shrugged. She had done that before and it had always been nothing, though normally it was Dawn who noticed the minute differences rather than one of her brothers.

"I'll make it in this afternoon. You better catch up with Roni and see if she's going to keep allowing you to live. I'll tell Dawn to expect the two of you at the Lawrences' cabin later. You won't be able to keep her away any longer."

"Yeah, I figured that one out already," he growled in irritation. "I'm going to snap someone's neck in two for allowing the information out. As soon as she lets me know just how the hell she found out."

Sherra grinned back at him in amusement. It was funny. Taber had always been one of the calmest of the Breeds until the past year. Just as with Callan, the responsibility of protecting the women they had claimed, and the unborn children resulting from it, was stretching all their nerves to a breaking point.

"Good luck then." She paused long enough to pat his shoulder before pulling the front door open and heading into the bright, crisp, clean air of the early fall day. The leaves were a hundred shades of brown, red and green as they prepared for the dormancy to come. The colors were dazzling to the eye and, not for the first time, filled Sherra with a sense of amazement.

It was more vivid today than it ever had been, though. She could feel a new sense of energy filling her, whipping through her body, and though she had just spent the night and early morning hours screaming beneath the fierce thrusts of Kane's body, she realized she still desired him. Still needed him.

It wasn't the burning, painful ache that it had been, rather it was a reminder, a pulsing echo that vibrated through her body and made her remember the night past with a small shiver of longing.

A small beep at her ear warned her that access to her personal channel was being requested. She reached up, flipping the switch that would block everyone but the person requesting a private conversation.

"Hey, gorgeous." Kane's voice filled her head, soft, amused, his voice heavy with the memories of the night they had shared.

Sherra smiled, shaking her head at that tone of voice.

"You're supposed to be working, stud," she reminded him, almost laughing at the memory of how that one little word could set his libido on fire.

"Oh, you're bad," he chuckled. "I might have to spank you."

"Mmm." She smiled as she moved across the compound, her steps light, filled with an energy she hadn't known she could feel. "Sounds interesting. Maybe I could spank you next, though. I think you'd like that, Kane."

"Probably too much." She could hear the rueful resignation in his voice. "Baby, if your hand is delivering it, I'm sure I couldn't help but enjoy it. What's your schedule today?"

"Patrol," she told him as she reached the small parking lot and the off-road Jeeps parked there. "I'll be on the west sector providing support as we search some of the caves there for tunnels leading through the mountains. We don't need anymore missile-toting assassins to come calling anytime soon."

Kane snorted at that. "Keep your people out of those caves and let the explosives crew take care of it. We don't need any more problems if they've wired the caverns too. The intel we finally received show some serious security weaknesses there. They would have to guess we'd find them eventually. Don't take chances."

Sherra rolled her eyes at the protectiveness in his tone.

"I'm a big girl, Kane, I know the rules," she reminded him, smiling for no other reason than the sound of his voice lightened her heart. "I promise to be a good girl."

"I'll meet you in a few hours and we'll sneak off somewhere for lunch and you can show me just how good you can be," he suggested, his voice wicked. "I'll provide the main course, you can provide the dessert." His voice dropped, grew husky and filled with sexual promise.

Sherra paused beside the Jeep, staring into the clear morning sky, a smile on her lips as Kane filled a part of her she didn't know existed. She could feel warmth blooming in her heart, heat in her pussy. She wanted him now, not later.

She shook her head at that thought and stepped into the Jeep.

"Get hold of me first," she told him as she started the engine and reversed the vehicle from its parking slot. "We might have to forgo food for dessert if things are too busy."

"Will do." She could hear the anticipation, the smile that filled his voice. "Be careful, kitty-mine. See you soon."

"Soon," she whispered in reply as the connection broke and the receiver automatically switched back to the primary channel.

She headed the Jeep to the back of the property and the high gate that guarded the back entrance. The day was looking brighter than ever.

"Sherra, I have my team ready to tackle these caves. When do you intend to give the go-ahead?"

Sherra hid her smile as Jonas Wyatt stalked through the clearing outside the caves in question, his dark face tightened into lines of impatient male arrogance, his light gray eyes flashing in demand.

He was going to be a hard one to handle. He had been in Sanctuary only a few months and already he was moving through the Alpha ranks. He had already fought or connived his way to team leader several times over until his rank was only just below that of the main Pride members and Kane's main team.

He was quick, efficient, and cold as ice.

"Sorry I'm late, Jonas." She hid her smile as she faced him, refusing to be drawn into a confrontation with him. The alpha genes that raged in that man's blood were like a virus eating him up. He wouldn't stop until he ruled his own little corner of the world. She just wished he would hurry up and stake that corner out and get off her back.

It was obvious it grated on his male pride, answering to a woman. Had it been Callan, or even Kane, he would have accepted it easier, but his natural male aggressions seemed to be assuring him that he had no place below her. She found him amusing. He found her irritating.

"Late is an understatement," he murmured as he came upon her, facing her with narrowed eyes and thin lips. "The day is going to be gone before we get the main tunnels covered. The last thing we need are more of those bastards slipping through."

She stopped, propping her hands on her hips and stared around the clearing, evaluating the team members, equipment, and quickly assessing and prioritizing what needed to be done.

"Let's get started." She breathed in deeply. "Watch for…"

"Wires, sound sensors and heat activators," he growled. "I know my job."

"Then do it," she griped in return. "Damn, Jonas, it's not like I'm trying to take your place here. You're team leader, big boy, go for it."

Surprise flashed in the narrowed eyes.

"I have two of my teams in there already," he grunted, surprising her now. "I was tired of waiting."

Sherra shook her head, a smile twitching her lips. "I'm going to begin suspecting you and Kane Tyler of being separated at birth."

"I might have to fight you over that insult," he growled. "Are you going in or supervising? I need to know before the rest of the teams move in."

"I'm going in. I'm trained in explosives detection and deactivation. We'll keep to the main tunnels for now and re-access in six hours. If there are as many tunnels as initial analysis is showing then we're going to have a hell of a job in front of us."

"More possibly." He nodded sharply. "Gear up. We're using Alpha Six channel but the tunnels are hampering reception without amplifiers in place. Be sure you pack a few."

She nodded quickly. "Let's head in then."

* * * * *

"Dammit, Sherra, I told you to keep your people out of these damned caves." Kane was furious as he confronted her in the main cavern of the cave system. As with the cave the assassin had used to slip onto the mountain, this one, too, had an extensive, mazelike tunnel system that burrowed beneath the mountain. And it had obviously been used, more than once, and in the last few days. Human scent filled it, even to the deepest portions of the tunnels that they had managed to access so far. Whatever intel they had received hadn't come close to the underground maze they had found here. And they had yet to find the exit on the other side.

Sherra rose from where she had been investigating the prints found in the tunnel she had taken. They were fresh, too damned fresh to suit her concerning the fact that here, the scent of intrusion was barely perceptible.

"And I told you to chill out," she grunted as he rounded the curve behind her, the scent of his arousal and his anger nearly causing her to stagger as it wrapped around her, reminding her of the craving that tormented her as well.

"Wrong answer," he barked furiously as he drew beside her and gripped her hip to stop her advance into one of the narrow tunnels. "Are you insane? Do you have any idea just how well these caves could be booby-trapped?"

She frowned, staring up into his furious face through the glow of the flashlight that was directed at the floor.

"Oh, I don't know, Kane," she responded with false sweetness. "Do you think the two explosives we dismantled an hour ago might have let me in on that little problem?"

So far, the two main tunnels they had found had been wired with enough explosives to bring the mountain itself down. They were expertly hidden and almost undetectable. Thankfully, Sherra, as well as several of the other Breeds, had been trained to detect explosives that some Breeds might miss. It wasn't so much as detecting the scent of the explosive itself as it was detecting the variance of the scents in the area of it.

When anything new was introduced into an area, even if its scent wasn't detectable to sensitive noses, the differences in the smells around them changed. This was how the two explosives had been found so far. Attempts had been made to camouflage the smell of the high-tech ingredients of the compound itself, which proved they had been set as a strike against the Breeds. Whether they were set before the Council evacuated or after, was anyone's guess at this point.

"Sherra, get the hell out of here." He stopped her again as she started to continue down the dirt path that led through the stone. "We'll get another explosives team out here…"

"What the hell do you think I am?" she asked him incredulously. "You've read my file, you know my training. I'm more than qualified to be here."

"You're more than stubborn and intractable, is what the hell you are."

He restrained her again, pushing her against the stone wall as he loomed over her. "I gave you a direct order, Sherra. Clear the fuck out."

She looked up at him slowly. "You must have me confused with someone who actually cares if they follow your orders, Kane," she said softly. "I don't."

"Don't care? Hell, I already know you don't follow my damned orders." He was literally baring his teeth now as he moved faster than she could defend against, shackling her hands to the wall as the flashlight fell to the floor, its dim glow enough to see the lust and fury raging in his gaze.

"Don't push me, Kane." She stared back at him relentlessly. "I won't be intimidated by you. Not now, not ever. I'm not some helpless little normal woman to bow and scrape at your feet for whatever order you would give."

"Who is head of security here, sweet thing?" He gave her a tight, hard grin. "Last I heard it wasn't you."

She sniffed at that. "Only because you have balls and I don't," she growled. "For some reason, Callan must think the size of your dick indicates your brain capacity. Perhaps I should warn him otherwise."

The truth was, Kane was better at the job and she knew it. But that didn't mean she didn't have her own strengths. Strengths she wouldn't allow him to take from her. She stared back at him mutinously, daring him to go any further in his male superior demands.

"Perhaps you should," he drawled. "But let's first see if the size of my dick can pound any sense into your stubborn ass first."

She had time to open her mouth with every intention of blasting him to hell and back with any and every insult she could pull out of her overheated brain, when his lips covered hers. There was a second of stunned surprise, that moment when she wondered why the hell she fought him, because the feel of his lips on hers was paradise.

This was the answer to every aching, hungry cell in her body. Her arms crossed over his shoulders, her fingers digging into the smooth muscle beneath his shirt as she slipped her tongue over his, following it as it retreated back into his mouth until his lips could close on her, suckling her tongue, drawing the sweet essence of the arousing hormone from the glands there and consuming it himself.

They both moaned, the sound trapped by the other's mouth as they ate at each other, lips and tongues meshed, pressing together as the carnality of the act became overwhelming.

Sherra could feel her pussy weeping, dampening her panties, making her move against the hard thigh that had slipped between hers, pressing against her cunt and setting it on fire.

"Dessert first," Kane growled as he tore his lips from hers, his hands moving to his jeans, releasing the material quickly. "Get out of those pants, Sherra, I can't wait much longer."

Feverish, enflamed, the sexuality spiraling between them was too hot, too intense to deny now. Her hands moved to the clasp of her own pants when she saw his cock revealed. His hand gripped it, fingers moving over it as he watched her from narrowed eyes.

Her fingers were trembling, her breath rasping in her throat as she pushed the waistband over her hips, the curve of her rear.

"I can't wait, Sherra," he whispered brokenly as he turned her. "Bend over. Put your hands against the wall."

He positioned her as he wanted her, bent, braced against the stone, as he spread her thighs as far as her pants allowed.

"Kane," she whimpered hungrily as she felt him bend, the blunt head of his erection sliding against the slick flesh of her over-sensitized pussy.

"Damn, baby, you're so hot," he whispered, one hand gripping her hip as he pulled at her, forcing her to rise to her tiptoes, to create the height needed to lodge the flared head at the entrance to her vagina. "There, Sherra," he groaned. "Hell yes, baby. Just like this."

She had to bite her lip to keep from screaming as he began to bore inside her. Slow rotations of his hips worked the hard flesh inside the gripping tissue of her pussy as she fought to breathe through the pleasure streaking through her.

"Trying not to scream, baby?" he asked her tightly, both hands at her hips now as he screwed inside her.

Sherra couldn't believe the eroticism of the act. Bent over, her pants at her ankles as Kane fucked her from behind, his cock worked inside her with rhythmic, powerful strokes that had her praying she wouldn't scream from need of him.

"You're cruel," she groaned, resting her head on her arm as she thrust her pussy on the smooth impalement. "Don't tease me like this, Kane."

"Oh, baby, that's not teasing," he assured her gently. "Now this, darlin', this is teasing."

She moaned helplessly as the strokes slowed but were no less devastating. Sweat began to dampen her body as electricity sizzled along her nerve endings. She panted, whimpered pleadingly, all in vain as Kane whispered his joy of her. How hot. How sweet. How tight...

She tasted blood as she bit her lip, fighting against his hold as she began to crave the deep, driving thrusts she knew he could give her. She wanted him slamming inside her, throwing her into the near violent orgasms that overtook her when he did so.

Instead, it was slow, measured thrusts. Deep, gentle penetrations that stretched the snug muscles and had her gripping him with a cry of longing, pulsing around his cock as he came over her, his lips settling on her neck.

"Kane, I can't stand it," she groaned as he retreated, returned, paused and retreated again only to renew the cycle.

"You have to stand it," he panted. "It's killing me, Sherra. You're killing me with pleasure and I can't stand the thought of letting you go."

He was pumping inside her, smooth, strong thrusts that were too slow, too damned teasing and only built her need higher. She was gasping for breath, her hips writhing as he restrained her, her pussy clenching convulsively around the steel-hard shaft driving her insane.

"If you don't fuck me, I swear I'll castrate you later," she groaned as his hips twisted, his hand lifting her as he sank deeper inside the burning depths of her vagina. "I mean it, Kane," she cried out. "I can't stand it. I need it harder."

"Ahh, baby, all you had to do was ask," he groaned, his own voice strained now as the pace increased.

Sherra felt her breath catch in her chest as her eyes closed helplessly. All her senses were centered between her thighs. The feel of his cock shafting her with hard, digging strokes, raking over sensitive tissue, stretching it, setting her on fire as he began, finally, to fuck her in earnest.

Their moans mingled in the dark confines of the tunnel, whispered gasps, female Feline growls of hunger merging in a symphony of lust and need.

Sherra moved back to him, driving him inside her, deeper, harder, feeling the smooth expanse of his cock head butting against her cervix as the knot of tension began to build within her womb. She was shaking, her legs trembling, her muscles tightening as Kane's pace increased further.

The sound of damp flesh smacking together, the sucking of her pussy around his cock all combined with the moans and filled her head with a screaming demand she knew she could no longer deny.

Her fingers clawed at the stone, her back arched as she drove herself harder on the wedge of flesh parting her, pistoning inside her now with hard, powerful strokes. A low cry built in her throat, then grew in volume as the conflagration of pleasure suddenly exploded from her womb and rushed through her body.

Kane was only a few strokes behind her. His teeth raked her neck as he drove in deep, then he bit her—he actually bit her—making her scream as another surge of violent reaction overtook her, shuddering through her body, bowing her back as she felt Kane's cock pulse, his semen, hot and rich, spew inside her.

"We're going to kill each other like this." He was breathing roughly long minutes later as he steadied her before weakly adjusting his pants and then helping her with hers.

Her hands were shaking, her body still racked by occasional shudders of pleasure as the echo of her orgasm worked through her.

"Yeah well, I did try to warn you." She tried to inject a small measure of waspishness into her tone, but it was impossible with the languor stealing over her. Damn, she could sleep now if there was a bed handy.

She drew in a deep, relaxing breath, then stilled. She felt her heart suddenly race in her chest, fear exploding in the pit of her stomach.

"What is it?" Kane rose from picking up the flashlight.

She turned, drawing in the scents from one end of the tunnel, then from the other.

"Fuck," she whispered. "Let's go. Fast. Somehow we've triggered an explosive."

It was close, but she didn't know how close. She could smell the damned thing heating up, preparing to blow, and knew there wasn't a chance in hell of finding it. According to the strength of the explosives it could be contained behind them, or the force of it could blow out the rest of the tunnel. With her and Kane inside it.

They ran.

Chapter Twelve

The blast of the explosion sent Sherra and Kane hurtling through the main cave opening, the sense of sudden weightlessness, of flight, was almost terrifying as she saw the boulders that surrounded the area looming below her. She tucked her body as she landed, rolled and came to her feet as she fought to catch her breath.

Kane was on his knees, choking against the dust settling around him as he too fought to get his bearings and to clear his head.

"Jonas," she yelled furiously as the Feline breeds rushed around them. "Head count. I need a head count." There had been others in the main cavern, as well as several of the smaller tunnels earlier.

"Everyone accounted for, Sherra," Jonas Wyatt called back, his voice cold, furious. "I have an ASAP out to a medic and Callan. Are you okay?"

"Do we have wounded?" She narrowed her eyes, seeing several Breeds sitting on the ground as the others attended them. "Status."

He jumped up from examining Kane, his gray eyes almost a quicksilver now with rage as he stared back at her, his face coated with grime, several scratches on his cheek where debris had obviously caught him. "We had major debris collapsing from above the mine entrance, we have minor injuries, a few broken bones. What the hell triggered that explosive?"

Alpha males, Sherra thought irrationally. Jonas Wyatt was one of the worst, easygoing one moment, taking charge the next. She saw now why he was rapidly rising within the security ranks at Sanctuary.

"Hell." She was breathing roughly, drawing in deep gulps of oxygen as Kane stumbled to his feet. "It must have been wired for sound. There was no scent of it, no sign of it, Jonas, before it started heating up. I'm starting to wonder if the whole system isn't one big grave in there."

Kane snorted sarcastically, though she fought to ignore him.

"Callan is arriving," Jonas called out as the sound of jeeps racing through the rough track up the mountain could be heard. "Get ready to move the wounded out. Sherra, do we stay or go?"

"You fucking go!" Kane turned on the Lion Breed furiously then. "Pack your shit up and get back to the compound. Now!"

Jonas blinked at him with a blank look. This was a Breed that rarely took orders, even from Callan. "Yes, sir." He finally nodded before turning away from him. "Load up, boys and girls, we're being sent home."

Kane was growling. Sherra tilted her head, watching him curiously as he kicked a stone, muttered something and flashed her another dangerous look.

She smiled brightly. "Ain't adrenaline a fine thing? Want to fuck it off?"

He frowned, lifted his lip in a violent portrayal of fury and stomped over to where Callan had pulled up in the pickup, followed by several Jeeps.

As she watched, Jonas sidled up to her. "Can humans be infected and turn Breed?" he asked her curiously. "I swear, I think he growls better than I do."

She stifled her laughter, elbowed the snickering Breed and hurried over to Callan. Only God knew what Kane was telling on her now.

Kane was definitely telling. Sherra snickered as Callan cast her a brooding look, questioned Kane, then nodded abruptly as she moved close enough to hear what they were saying.

"The caves are obviously a trap. Best case, we blow all the entrances until this situation eases and we can complete the intel and find the entrances the terrorists are using. Until then, we're sitting ducks or dead in those mazes, your pick." Kane's voice was weary, strained. "I can't see the sense in risking our men and women this way, Callan."

Sherra stood behind him, her amusement wiped away by the sound of his voice, the tension filling him. It wasn't sexual, it was exhausted.

Callan stared around the area, watching as the wounded were quickly loaded to the backs of the jeeps for transportation back to the clinic.

"Blow them," Callan gave the order, his voice low, throbbing with anger. "They're not worth trying to keep considering the risk."

Sherra watched as Kane breathed in roughly, shaking his head as he stared to his side, watching the Breeds clear the area as Jonas began inspecting the now-sealed entrance. Kane's shoulders were tense, tight, as he shrugged them with an appearance of weariness. She gave Callan a narrow-eyed look.

He stared back at her for long moments before his gaze flickered back to Kane.

"Let's head back." He pushed his fingers through his thick fall of hair, breathing out in irritation. "We're expecting more information in on the Purist group rumored to be gathering. Alexandria and I want to be there when the report comes in. And you and Sherra, neither one look in peak condition. Have you two forgotten how to fucking sleep?"

Kane glanced back at Sherra, his eyes dark, concerned. She barely kept from rolling her eyes.

"I am tired," she finally admitted, breaking the contact as she stared back at her brother. "This shit is getting to me, Callan. We have to do something."

"Agreed," Callan grunted. "When you find an answer be sure to let me know, because I'll be damned if I've come up with one yet. By the way, they released our friendly neighborhood missile launcher this morning. Some pansy-assed judge dropped the charges slick as you please."

Sherra closed her eyes, hearing Kane's vicious curse at this news.

"Joy, joy," she murmured. "Next one, I'll just kill and get it over with." She wasn't joking.

"I'll help you hide the body." The cold smile twisting Kane's lips was almost scary to see. But what worried her more was the pale cast to his sun-darkened features.

"Come on, stud." She moved to his side, butting against his arm as she let her own weariness show on her face. Something she abhorred. "I don't know about you, but a shower is definitely called for, and a nap."

His arm went around her waist instantly, his hand cupping her hip as he dragged her against his chest, the muscles tight as he held her to him.

"I'm going to paddle your ass for being in that damned cave," he suddenly snapped, his eyes glittering with barely suppressed fury.

She did roll her eyes, seeing more than just his anger. She hated seeing the emotions that tore at him, blazing in his eyes, in the tight features of his face. It reminded her forcefully of the ties they shared, the pain he had suffered because of her, for her. And that reminder had the power to weaken her as nothing else did.

The gentle aura of the morning had faded with the danger surrounding them once again, but nothing could extinguish her need for him. She could excuse them on lust all she wanted to, but at her weakest moments, such as now, she knew the truth. Loving him was killing her. Not because she couldn't have him—she could, she did. But the past was a cruel specter that haunted her, snatching sleep from her, terrifying her with the weaknesses she knew she possessed. Weaknesses she couldn't let him see, couldn't let him know.

"Come on, Kane, let's go home," she sighed, moving slowly from him, her body dragging, exhaustion pulling at her as she headed for her jeep. She needed to sleep, just once, without arousal destroying her, or memories tormenting her. Just once.

* * * * *

Kane could feel his flesh sensitizing in ways he had never expected. He couldn't understand it, couldn't explain it. He paced outside Sherra's bathroom after their return to the compound, running his hand over his hair as he fought the insane compulsion to storm into her shower and take her where she stood. He needed his cock buried inside her heat, and he needed it now.

He shook his head. Even after that first kiss it hadn't been like this. This was consuming, an urgent compulsion, a desire unlike anything he had known to this point. He tried to explain the sensation away on the fact that they had nearly died in those damned caves earlier, but there was no logic in that. There was no way to explain the sudden surge of lust that burned brighter, hotter than anything he had ever known before this point.

God help them both if she had any intentions of refusing him, because he didn't think he could leave her. He knew he couldn't deny the hunger for her. He could taste her on his tongue, craved the feel of her against his flesh.

He shrugged his broad, bare shoulders, the caress of the air generated against his flesh had him flinching at the sensation. Dammit, a man shouldn't be that sensitive.

The shower shut off and he tensed in preparation. He could imagine her—her flesh all slick and wet, creamy and pink and more tempting than anything he knew. He still remembered the feel of her in that cave. Her kiss had tasted more delicate, the spice of the hormone filling his senses as he fought to keep some measure of sanity.

His cock had still been hard when he pulled from her. Even after spilling himself inside her with a violence he hadn't known a man was capable of, he still needed more of her.

He turned away from the bathroom door, pacing the floor, trying to make sense of his emotions and the strange feelings moving through him. He wanted so much. Things he had never thought of before, never considered.

Damn, he loved her. That was the one thing that had always been a constant in his life, but he was starting to feel as though the mating heat and the sex alone was all that bound them. And that was the crux of the matter.

He winced at the knowledge. He had lived to avenge her all these years, had fought to find justice for the woman he thought he had lost, only to feel his world brighten once again when he found her. He hadn't allowed his confidence to be dented by her anger or feigned hatred. He hadn't let her resentment sway him. She belonged to him, heart and soul.

"Damn." He sat down on the chair in the corner of the room and braced his elbows on his knees as he covered his face with his hands. Why hadn't he noticed this before? Why hadn't he seen what was happening?

"I warned you there was little satisfaction to be had, Kane." Sherra stood in the doorway, a towel covering her lithe body, her long hair damp and framing her somber face.

He grimaced at the words, giving his head a quick jerk as he stared back at her and for the first time, he saw her. Her shoulders were tightened defensively, her eyes wary, always watching.

"Is the heat easing for you?" he asked her.

She shrugged negligently. "It's in its last phases."

"Have you seen the doc?" He knew she hadn't.

"Not yet. I'll go in the morning," she assured him, faint confusion showing in her expression.

"You told Taber you'd go in tonight," he reminded her. "I'll be waiting on you in the doctor's office in the morning."

He rose to his feet, suddenly tired. Despite the hard-on making him crazy and the hunger eating away at his soul, he felt old. Shaking his head, he moved to the door and opened it slowly.

"Kane?" He paused, keeping his back to her, knowing if he looked at her he would go to her, touch her, take her. And once again the truth would eat him alive.

"Yeah, babe?" He kept his voice soft, hoping to hide the regret.

"You aren't staying?" she asked, her tone equally soft, though confused.

He drew in a deep, hard breath. "Not tonight, Sherra. If you need me, you know where to find me."

The silence behind him was louder than fury could have been. He tapped his fist against the doorframe as he kicked himself. Damn, he'd made more of a mess of this than he had the first time around.

"Night, Sherra." He left her bedroom, ignoring his arousal, the pain slicing through his chest, and realized that perhaps the love he had seen in her so long ago truly had died.

God he was fucking tired. He hung around this damned compound like a puppy nipping at her heels demanding her affection. It was senseless and was beginning to grate on his pride daily. He hadn't betrayed her, he hadn't left her in that hellhole deliberately. If he had things to do over, he would have never left her there while he went for help, he would have taken her, despite the risks. But the past couldn't be undone.

She blamed him for the loss of the baby. Hell, he couldn't blame her, he blamed himself, even though he had been unaware of the conception. That loss haunted him as few other things could. His child. His and Sherra's.

He shook his head as he entered his bedroom. Sitting on his bed he pulled his boots from his feet, then rose to shed his clothes before lying back on the bed. His fingers wrapped around his cock, stroking over it slowly as his eyes closed and imagined her, touching him.

A grim smile tugged at his lips. Her hands were softer than silk, warmer than fire. She could bring him to his knees with a smile, make his heart and his dick swell with no more than a look from those gorgeous green cat's eyes. And her body. His groan was low, hungry. Her body made him sweat with lust. All sweet curves and satiny warmth that beckoned and drove a man mad with the need to fuck.

His fingers quickened on his erection as his mind filled in the blanks. Syrup-sweet juices coated her soft pussy, hard nipples topping firm breasts as his tongue stroked them, sucked them into his mouth. His fingers dipping into her cunt, hearing her hot little moans in the air around them as he fucked her easily, pushing into her, feeling her stretch around him as she cried out her need.

His balls tightened, his thighs bunching as a low growl left his lips and his semen spurted from his cock. It eased the ache, left him gasping, still hungry, but he prayed, relaxed enough to sleep.

He rolled over, burying his head in his pillow and tried to ignore the fact that once again, he slept alone.

Sherra stared at the door in bemusement. What the hell had happened? Had he cracked his head during the explosion? And what the hell did he mean that she knew where to find him? Since when did he expect her to find him? He had been on her ass since finding her in Sandy Hook, never letting up and damned sure never giving up.

She propped her hands on her hips, more confused now than she ever had been. She had smelled his arousal, hotter, more demanding than it had ever been. And he had just walked away.

She turned from him. Pulling the towel from her body, she threw it into the bathroom before dressing in a long caftan and quietly leaving her room. She padded downstairs, drawn by Callan and Merinus' voices in the kitchen and a need for advice.

Advice wasn't something she usually looked for. She had tried, over the years, to burden Callan the least amount possible with her own problems, knowing that the protection of the Pride was more important.

"Hi, Sherra, I thought you had retired for the night." Merinus smiled as she sipped a glass of cold milk.

Sherra watched her with a faint grin.

"I see you found the Oreos Kane sneaked in for Cassie."

Merinus grinned in conspiracy. "I knew he would do it. Kane's kept me in cookies all my life."

Sherra frowned at that as she looked at Callan. "Why don't *you* buy her cookies? You're not exactly a pauper, you know."

Callan grinned as he leaned back in his chair, his fingers playing with his wife's hair as he watched his sister.

"It pleases him to provide them and allows him to retain a feeling of possessiveness. Why would I take that from him? Kane's protected her all her life, cared for her, even now. I don't have a problem with the cookies." Callan shrugged carelessly.

Sherra looked at her brother oddly.

"But she's *your* wife," she stressed. "Your responsibility."

Callan's eyes narrowed thoughtfully for a moment. He was her beloved older brother, but she could see where Merinus had been unable to refuse the story once she saw his picture. He was exceptionally handsome in a rough sort of way. High cheekbones, a narrow, savage face. Sensual lips. He had the Lion's cast to his face, but it didn't detract from his looks in the least.

"She is." He nodded. "But Kane was a part of her life first. And for longer. Why should I resent or interfere in the relationship that he cherishes so dearly?"

Merinus hadn't said anything. She dipped her Oreos placidly in the glass of milk and watched Sherra with eyes that were far too knowing.

Sherra shrugged. "I was just curious."

"You are never just curious, Sherra," he reflected. "What's the problem? You're still in heat, yet you stand here asking me questions rather than taking time to bond with your mate."

She stilled, blinking over at him in confusion. "It's sexual…"

Callan breathed out heavily. "Sherra." He shook his head. "I won't argue your beliefs with you, though I highly disagree. The heat isn't just physical, I've warned you of this."

He had. He had lectured on emotional, physical, and spiritual bondings. It hadn't made sense then, and it didn't make sense now.

She hunched her shoulder as she walked over to the doors that led to the sheltered grotto outside.

"So where is Kane?" Merinus asked casually, though Sherra could hear the hint of anger warming her voice.

She shrugged. "His room, I believe."

"And you're here, why?" Merinus asked. "What happened?"

She turned back to them, frowning in confusion. "I don't know. I came out of the bath and he appeared…almost sad…melancholy, as though the weight on his shoulders was too heavy to bear. I assumed the heat was the cause and reminded him that I had warned him of the consequences." She looked to her brother, frowning as she tugged at her lower lip with her teeth. "He just walked away, Callan. I can't understand why he just walked away."

Callan grimaced. "Kane is different, Sherra. You can't see him as you do me, or one of the others. In many ways, his life has been just as hard, the inner scars as deep as the outer. Perhaps you should ask him."

"He wouldn't tell her," Merinus said at that point, leaning back in her chair and laying her hands on her distended abdomen.

Sherra frowned over at her. "Why not?"

"Because you should know. You know him better than you think you do, Sherra. You're just trying to deny that you don't." Merinus shrugged as her hands smoothed over the light blue cotton smock she wore. "Besides, if he thought you didn't know what the problem was, then he wouldn't have hesitated to tell you."

"So I'm supposed to read his mind now?" Sherra growled. "The man is the most exasperating, confusing male I have ever met in my life, Merinus. How am I supposed to know what goes on in his brain?"

He was going to drive her insane.

"Kane's brain isn't what you should be worrying about," Merinus assured her. "From the way you said he was acting, you've hurt him, Sherra. Somehow, you've hurt him deeply."

Emotion glittered in the other woman's eyes, a sheen of tears that caused Sherra's heart to clench. In all their conversations about Kane, Merinus had never shed tears. Why would she now?

"How could I have hurt him?" She spread her hands wide in confusion. "I didn't *do* anything, Merinus."

Merinus' look was hard, cold. "Evidently you did do something. You defeated Kane. And until now, I could have sworn no one could." With the help of her mate she rose to her feet, her gaze never leaving Sherra's. "If I lose my brother because you're too damned stubborn to admit the truth to yourself, then I'll never forgive you. Remember that one, sister-in-law."

She leaned down and kissed Callan lingeringly. "Come to bed soon. I miss you when you're not there."

He touched her face. It was a curiously gentle gesture, his fingertips sliding over her cheek as though he enjoyed the touch of her skin.

"Love you, babe," he whispered.

"Love you back." Merinus' fingers trailed over his shoulder as she waddled past him and headed for the elevator in the hall outside the kitchen.

"You seem confused, Sherra," Callan grunted as he rose from the table, collecting Merinus' saucer and glass and taking them to the sink.

Sherra shrugged. Kane was often reaching out to touch her as Merinus had Callan. Light, gentle caresses. An affirmation that he was truly with her.

His gaze filled with wonder as his fingertips reached for her cheek. She flinched at the memory just as she flinched when he tried to touch her like that. Not because she didn't want him to, because each time he did, something softened inside her. Something that made her hungrier, made her need him more.

"How do you know it's love and not just chemistry?" she whispered as she rubbed her arms, watching her brother as he rinsed his wife's glass and saucer and put them in the dishwasher. "It could just be the heat, Callan," she told him desperately. "What happens when it fades?"

"The heat goes away, Sherra, you know that," he berated her. "Your body is trying to tell you what your heart and mind have already accepted. You're just too stubborn to listen to it."

She almost gaped at him. "How can you say that? Callan, this isn't stubbornness." She tried to hide the pain his words caused—even more, she tried to hide from the sense of truth that exploded in her chest.

He leaned against the counter, crossing his arms over his chest. "He's a hard man. A prick if one was ever born. But he's a good man, Sherra. And despite his sarcasm and mockery, he shows the people he considers his how much he cares in the only way he knows how. Telling yourself you don't love him won't help. I know you do. I've known it since I first saw the two of you together. Maybe you should accept it now."

Chapter Thirteen

It was disconcerting, realizing the battle she had been waging had been a lie. As Sherra stood on her balcony, staring into the darkness, she admitted the truth to herself. She *had* been concerned about the effects of the Mating Heat on Kane, that hadn't been so much a lie as it had been a cover. If she focused on that, then she didn't have to look at herself or her own fears.

Loving him again wasn't the problem. She had always loved him. From the moment she first saw him at the Labs, her heart had belonged to him. It was admitting that love and allowing the defenses which had protected her over the years, to disintegrate. Defenses that had kept her strong, that had kept her from losing her mind during those dark, pain-hazed days before Callan had effected their escape.

She had convinced herself she didn't love, that she hated. When she could no longer hate, she had held onto the belief that she didn't love. But she did. Until she felt as though she would shatter from the inside out, she loved Kane Tyler. And that was a weakness. The worst weakness of all.

She had nearly died the first time she lost him. During those first days, when Dayan had convinced her that Kane had walked away, that he was never coming back, she had wanted to die. Until she realized she carried his child. The thought of that baby had strengthened her, had brought her back from a brink that terrified her now. It had allowed her time to convince herself she hated him, that she didn't need him. When she lost the baby, that hatred had fortified her. Had helped her survive. She would live simply because he hadn't given a damn one way or the other if she did.

Now what? The lies she had used to protect herself were gone. There was only Kane now. And whatever love he had for her, she was destroying with her own stubbornness.

A low, agonized growl left her throat as she turned from the balcony and paced the room. She ached for him. Ached until she thought her soul would shatter from the need, and yet, she couldn't force herself to go to him, couldn't give him whatever words he seemed to need.

There was no relief. No Kane. She was confined to the house for whatever reasons, not that she believed the excuses he made for even a moment. There were plenty of guards within the house if another attack occurred. He wanted her close, wanted to protect her, shelter her. Smother her.

She could feel her chest tightening with the knowledge. He wanted to touch her, not just for sex, but because he needed that touch. And she withheld every desire she had to do the same.

Why? Why was she so stubborn, so damned dead set against the intimacies he wanted? That she knew she wanted herself.

Her breath hitched in her chest as the knowledge seared her. If she let herself accept, what happened if she lost him again? What happened if somehow, Kane were killed, or he grew tired of her? How would she survive then? That was the true barrier between her and Kane. It wasn't her concern, especially considering the fact there was no reason to be concerned. They were both in full mating heat, and she knew Kane's physical discomfort was even greater than her own now. It showed in the tension in his shoulders, the lack of sleep in his expression. He was killing himself. She was killing him.

She lowered her head, shivering as she stepped back onto the balcony, feeling the cold wind that whipped around her, but knowing the chill inside her came from much more than the weather.

She was destroying them both, and Kane deserved so much better than that. He deserved more than a woman whose dreams were often shattered by nightmares, whose heart was scarred by a past neither of them should be blamed for.

And yet, she was still blaming him. She breathed in roughly, fighting the tears that hovered just behind her eyes, that tightened her chest as the realization crystallized within her. She still blamed him, not just for leaving her, or the loss of their child, but for her own inability to get past the pain.

The sob that tore from her chest caught her unawares. The pain that ambushed her soul filled her heart, tearing at the promises she had made to herself over the years. All she remembered, all she felt were the needs. Not the sexual needs, the emotional. The desperation when darkness fell to be held, to know the warmth of his body, to feel his fingers stroking along her cheek...

He had done that once. She was only distantly aware of the soft sobs falling from her lips as she remembered the one time he had caressed her in such a way. Just before he had taken her that first time, knowing the cameras watched them, he had to have known, even if she didn't. His fingertips had smoothed over her cheek as he stared into her eyes.

"We play the game when we must." His voice had been so soft, so whisper-thin she had barely heard him. *"And we love however we can. I love you, Sherra..."*

She wrapped her arms over her breasts, the cries that filled her soul escaping as harsh whimpers as tears dampened her cheeks now. She hadn't flinched from him then, she remembered. That touch had echoed in her soul even before he spoke the words. And now, she denied them both the fulfillment that she knew could be found in only one manner. In the acceptance not just of the physical, but the emotional as well.

Denying him was doing her no good. She could excuse it until hell froze over, but if something happened to him, she would die anyway. Perhaps not physically, but just as she had until she saw him again, she would die inside.

Wiping furiously at her tears, she drew in a hard, desperate breath as she blinked back her tears. Kane was withdrawing, and if Merinus was right, then it was because he was losing hope, just as she had lost hope so many years before. They had been apart long enough. She had been alone so fucking long that she had forgotten why she hurt so deeply inside her soul. She hurt because Kane hadn't been there. Because he wasn't holding her, touching her, filling not just her body, but her heart.

But he was here now. This was the chance she had dreamed of in the darkest nights when she refused to acknowledge why she awoke crying. This was the chance she had prayed for in those dark days after the loss of the baby, when life hadn't seemed worth living.

She had lost enough. It was time to take what was hers, and Kane was hers.

* * * * *

"Keep the sensors outside the caves. We'll wire them for sound and visual and hopefully have more of a warning if another of the missile-toting bastards decides to come calling." Kane was hunched over satellite images of the land the Breeds owned as his unit stood around the briefing table in his room. "The images aren't showing the caves we're finding, but if you look damned close, you'll see a shadowing instead." He pointed out two of the areas where the almost imperceptible blurring occurred on the thick pages. "These images were very carefully 'fixed'. So far, I've found six areas that need to be checked. Get three more units together in the morning and get started finding the others. I'll brief Callan and Taber first thing in the morning."

"What about new images?" Jackal asked him softly, his smooth voice breaking in on Kane's thoughts. "The Army satellite that took these should have been able to give us an idea of where the caves exited on both sides, as well as an idea of their tunnel systems. What if we commission more images?"

Jackal was as calm and cold as the deepest winter night. He had been one of the first soldiers Kane had chosen for his team of rescue experts. He never became upset or irritated. Never raised his voice. If you pissed him off bad enough, you were dead. It was that simple and that quick.

"Same problem." Kane breathed out roughly as he fought to keep his thoughts straight.

He should have been comfortable right now, he thought furiously. Instead of chilling out with a beer and dressing in the soft gray sweatpants he preferred for evening, he was suffering in heavy jeans and the hard-on from hell.

"Not really," his technical expert, Ice, spoke up then. "Lawrence Industries has their own satellite orbiting Earth. Why not put the bastard to work after all the trouble he's caused breaking our gate like he did? If he's really serious about wanting to be a part of his sister's life, he'd get you what you need."

"How can we be sure it's reliable, though?" Jackal tapped the images they had impatiently. "Look how the government screwed these over."

"Because one of us would be there when the images download." Ice smiled coldly. "I know how to operate and program the satellites. If Lawrence would clear me for it, I could get everything we need."

Kane narrowed his eyes on the tall soldier. Ice had trained on some pretty advanced government systems before joining his team.

"Have Dawn approach him on it." Kane nodded, his eyes narrowing at the thought. Dawn was running from Lawrence, it was as plain as the fear on her face. "That could solve a lot of our problems right there. If he agrees, he'll move up on the personal scale of trust. If he tries to get out of it, he moves higher on the list of suspects. Personally, I think he'll be eager to help."

Seth Lawrence seemed sincere in his offers to help where he could and to make protecting his sister and future niece or nephew easier. So far, he had accepted his restrictions on the compound as well as the heavily guarded meetings he was being allowed with his sister. It grated on him, Kane could tell.

Having his motives questioned so intently wasn't something he liked, but he understood the motives behind it.

Kane felt like he was sending Dawn to a ravening wolf though. Seth Lawrence's interest in her wasn't hidden, nor was Dawn's intention of avoiding it. The damned women of this Pride were going to drive him to an early grave. Him and every other man in the compound if they weren't careful.

Kane rubbed the back of his neck, wishing he could relieve the tension in his body as easily.

"Okay, one problem down, how many more to go?" he asked impatiently.

"We have everything else covered," Jackal assured him. "One of us will work with a Breed unit for a while, but I'll tell you, those Breeds are hardheaded and slick as hell. I don't know if we have much to offer them in information or experience. Some of those boys are your worst nightmare. And I won't even mention those women. It's enough to make a man want to start executing Council members. And that Lion, Wyatt, would scare the bejeebies outta me if I were anyone else. If there's a weapon he doesn't know how to use or a situation he can't twist his way, then I don't know of it."

Kane knew exactly how he felt. The female Breeds were often the most dangerous. Their eyes were shadowed with nightmares, their dreams haunted by them. Some would go days without sleep rather than face the demons awaiting them. And Wyatt was a pain in the ass.

"We need a psychologist in here," he growled. "Callan's refusing so far, but I'm working on it."

He understood Callan's objections. If by some chance the psychologist was a Council sympathizer, they could do more harm than good. But some of the Breeds were walking a fine line with their sanity and their morals.

"You city boys and your psychologists," Jackal snorted. "Just what we need, some fancy-pants lolly-gaggin' around telling us all how we need to get in touch with our inner child," he sneered. "I find that little inner bastard and I'll choke the shit out of him for the hell of it."

"Are you having fun yet, Jackal?" Ice snickered as the broad ex-Kansas farm boy flashed him a killing look.

Jackal snorted. "Not yet. Want to volunteer as a punching bag there, Icy?"

"Enough." Kane didn't have time for their friendly bickering. "Move out," he told them as he rolled the images up and handed them back to Jackal. "Stay in regular touch and keep me up to date with your progress tomorrow. I'll talk to Lawrence first thing in the morning."

The other men filed out of the room, finally leaving Kane in blessed peace. The first thing he did was strip. If he didn't get his bound cock out of those damned jeans he knew he'd go crazy.

Naked, his cock engorged and heavy, he collapsed back in the chair on one side of the room and stared around in frustration.

He could be drilling his tortured erection inside the heated clasp of Sherra's cunt right now if he weren't so damned stubborn. He rested his head on the back of the chair, his fingers stroking over his cock as he imagined her tight, liquid heat flowing over his shaft to his balls and making his entire body tighten in the need to ejaculate inside her.

Unfortunately, it was never enough. Not physically. Physically, he understood the gnawing hunger. The hormone was building in his bloodstream in a manner that had the old doctor looking at him oddly again, and it was the cause of the unceasing sexual arousal. The insatiable longing that filled his soul was another matter, though. He frowned, scratching absently at his scarred chest at the thought. There was something missing, something that no matter how often he took Sherra, couldn't fill that steadily widening void.

Her heart. He blew his breath out heavily as he once again acknowledged the truth. He didn't have her heart. He had her body, the commitment of her fidelity, but it wasn't voluntary. And that was the killer. She was his only because of the chemistry between them.

There was none of the gentle touches or intimate rubbing of bodies as he had seen with the other Breeds and their mates. Sherra avoided that as much as possible. When they were together it was the sex she wanted and nothing more. And Kane needed more.

He moved his hands to the arms of the chair, his fingers clenching on them as he gritted his teeth in fury. How often had he tried to touch her, yearned to feel just the softness of her flesh against his fingertips, or the warmth of her body against him? More times than he cared to count, and in every instance she had flinched or moved carefully away from him. Each time he had been denied.

"Kane?" Sherra's voice outside his bedroom door had him frowning darkly.

You know where to find me if you need me. He had made the offer, so why did it grate now that she had come?

"It's unlocked." He didn't move from his nude, sprawled position in the chair. He lowered his head, watching as the panel swung open and she stepped carefully inside.

Chapter Fourteen

Damn, she looked like an angel. All that blonde hair, thick and lustrous, framed her face and fell down her back in a skein of pure white silk. The emerald-green caftan flowed over her body, whispering over her breasts, hips and thighs and falling to her graceful feet.

Her eyes widened at his aroused, nude state. Swallowing tightly, she closed the door and slid the lock home.

Kane narrowed his eyes on her then. She looked…uncomfortable. Her hands still gripped the doorknob, her eyes were dark with both arousal and trepidation. And something more, some emotion he couldn't put his finger on, couldn't define. Hell, she was probably going to tell him to take a flying leap and fuck himself. She had done it often enough in the past few months.

God knew there were days he wished he could. When he wished he could effect the distance she had forced between them and ignore the needs that ate at his gut like acid.

"It's a boner not a monster," he growled, waving a hand to the erection her gaze continued to flicker back and forth from. "You're watching it like you expect it to bite."

"It looks angry enough." A nervous little smile touched her lips before it fell and she watched him somberly. "*You* look angry enough."

He breathed out roughly in frustration. "I'm dead tired, Sherra, and horny to boot. If that's why you're here then come on."

He rose to his feet, eager to fill her, to still at least that part of his pain.

She bit her lip, her gaze flickering to the bed.

"That wasn't all I wanted," she whispered, her gaze meeting his, breaking his heart with the vulnerability he glimpsed there.

He rubbed at the back of his neck wearily. "What else could there be?" he finally asked. "I'll be honest, baby, my control and my patience are worn thin tonight, so this isn't a good time for a fight."

"But it's okay to fuck?" There was no heat in her voice, only that shattered soberness that made him ache clear to his soul.

God, he wanted to touch her. He wanted to just brush his fingertips over her cheek, nuzzle her jaw. He was worse than the frigging cat boys running around the damned place.

"Yeah." He swiped his hand over his hair. "It's okay to fuck."

It was better to fuck, his dick was screaming.

She lowered her head, nodding hesitantly though she made no move to either undress or head to the bed.

"Sherra, why the hell are you here?" he finally growled. "You're obviously not in any hurry to do the nasty here with me, so why not tell me what you do want?"

She bit her lip and he wanted to groan.

"I want to know why you're so angry," she finally said, lifting her eyes to him as she twisted her fingers together in front of her. "Why you walked out of my room and why you're acting more like an asshole than normal. I want you to talk to me, Kane."

He snorted, grimacing at the plea. "I've been talking to you for months now, Sherra, and you haven't bothered to listen. Why now?"

She glanced away before tucking a loose strand of hair behind her ear.

"You haven't walked away from me before, Kane." She sounded confused, as though the very act of him doing so had thrown her little world out of kilter.

Kane snorted a half laugh as his lips curved mockingly. He had chased after her like a lovesick dog after a bitch in heat, and the reason she was taking notice was that he had suddenly walked away. It was pissing him off.

"I told you I was here if you needed me." He finally shrugged as he moved to the bed, stretching out on it suggestively, his hand gripping the base of his cock as he watched her. "This is all you need from me, isn't it, baby? Come on and get it. It's all yours, anytime." He hated the fury throbbing in his chest, the need to shake her, to make her see once and for all everything she was throwing away.

She stared back at him in indecision, her expression filled with grief, with a pain that broke his heart.

"I don't know what to do, Kane," she whispered, the desperation in her voice echoing around them. "I don't know how to fix this, how to fix myself."

His clenched his teeth together at the helpless pain in her voice.

"I want you. I need you. I accept you as my mate. What more can I give you that you don't already have?" She stared at him, her voice ragged, confusion and anger filling her voice.

Her love. He sighed roughly. "I'm not asking you for anything more, Sherra," he finally said in resignation. What right did he have to ask her for shit? "Not anymore."

She moved slowly away from the door, stepping closer to him before stopping again.

"You're wanting something I'm not giving," she whispered. "I want to give it to you, Kane. I swear I do. I want you happy, I want you to know some peace as desperately as I need it for myself. Tell me what you want. Tell me what to do."

She was gripping her hands in front of her, her fingers twisting together as she stared at him out of those shadowed, pain-ridden eyes. God help him, she had hurt so much in her lifetime. Was it fair that she hurt even a second more than she had to? That she should hurt because of his failure to protect her?

"Sherra..." He whispered her name with bleak sadness. "Come here, baby." He held his hand out to her slowly. "You don't have to guess. There's nothing to tell. I think Taber's contagious. All those foul moods of his." He nearly choked on the words.

She shook her head desperately. "Don't lie to me now," she snapped, her eyes flashing with anger now. "Don't pacify me."

He reached up to touch her cheek, but allowed his hand to drop to her shoulder instead, covering his own need, his own betraying action.

He tried to smile. "I need you," he finally whispered. There was no need in making her pain greater at this moment. She gave him what she had, and it was more than he should expect, wasn't it?

Because of him she had lost their child, had been drugged and cruelly raped and forced to survive in fear for nearly a decade. Because he had failed.

She didn't want his tenderness, he knew. The gentle touches he would have given her, the soft words. She wanted to be fucked. She wanted the heat eased, wanted to be taken until her orgasm exploded through her body, relieving her of the pain. He could give her this, and if it failed to still his own hungers, then it was his fault, not hers.

"I dreamed of you for so many years," she whispered then, staring up at him, her eyes dark, creased with pain. "Even though I thought you betrayed me, I ached until I thought I would die from the need. Not the need to be fucked, but the need to be held." Her voice broke as a shudder racked her body. "I made myself hate, instead of love. I forced those needs so deep inside me that letting them go is as hard as forcing them down was to begin with."

He stilled, watching her quietly now, hearing the words, seeing the tears in her eyes as she blinked furiously. And hope filled his heart.

"You touch me, and I feel all those defenses cracking..." A small sob filled her voice then. "I feel all those hopes and dreams that almost killed me rising inside me again. And it terrifies me..." A tear dropped down her cheek, a silky track of pain that had his heart clenching. "What do I do?" Her hands pressed against his chest, small fists that thumped against the scars as rage flashed in her eyes. "God damn you, Kane, what do I do if I lose you again? How will I survive loving you this fucking much, more than I ever did before, if I lose you?"

Joy ripped through his soul as he stared back at her in disbelief. It was all there now, filling her eyes, as surely as the pain, confusion and emotion filled them. Tears ran unchecked down her cheeks as he reached up slowly, his fingertips touching them hesitantly as she held firm. She didn't flinch. Her eyes fluttered in pleasure as he smoothed the dampness away, her breath hitching as she stared back at him. Loved him.

"I loved you then, but never as much as I love you now," he whispered. "I knew what it was like to lose you, to believe there was no hope, no chance of ever touching you again, of feeling your warmth or your kiss. And even then, I fought for you. I fought your battle, and in the darkest dreams I raged at the loss. Until I saw you in the darkness, heard your voice, saw your eyes and I breathed again." His voice rasped from his throat as he fought back his own tears. "I die inside when I awake alone, always wondering if I dreamed you. If you were never really there. My first glimpse of you each morning is like a little slice of heaven. But I need more, Sherra." His thumb pressed against her lips, holding back her response until he could finish. "I need your heart. I need the same bond from you that I give to you. I can't live on hopes. Not like this."

"I love you," she sobbed. "What more do you want?"

"No more running." He gripped her shoulders, forcing himself to lighten his hold, his desperation. "No more fucking denials, Sherra. No more separate beds or hiding. All or nothing. I want it all."

"What the hell do you think I'm trying to give you, asshole?" She snarled in his face then, her canines flashing in warning as she growled the words. "Do you want me to take out a fucking ad or something?"

"I could handle that." He tilted his head as though considering the suggestion, holding back his smile, his laughter. His joy. "It would be a start."

Her eyes narrowed, anger flashing hot and deep an instant before she drew back her fist. He caught it just as quickly, laughed then pulled her to him. His lips covered hers as a strangled gasp left them. She was soft, delicate, her flesh warm and as tempting as sin itself as he moved quickly, lifting her to him as he fell back on the bed, pulling her along his body as his lips ate at hers, and she followed suit with a hunger that matched his own.

Kane flattened his hands, running them down the silk of the caftan to her hips. There, he bunched the material, pulling it up along her legs as they tangled with his, desperate to feel her naked flesh against him.

His lips fought for supremacy of their kiss, for once he didn't give a damn about that fucking hormone. She was his. Finally. Completely. Fuck that damned hormone.

His tongue plunged past her lips instead, tangling with hers, growling warningly when she tried to take control of the kiss. His hands moved to the neckline of the caftan, gripping the material and ripping it with a savage rend as he bore her to her back on the bed.

He struggled for control. He wanted it to last. He wanted her so damned hot, so out of her mind with the pleasure that she allowed him to love her. Allowed him to touch her, stroke her as he longed to.

She stared up at him, her cheeks flushed, her green eyes glittering now with excitement rather than pain as he rose over her, pulling the ruined gown from her body as he gazed at the skin he uncovered.

A light blush covered the smooth mounds of her swollen breasts. He ran the backs of the fingers of one hand over the nearest curve and almost trembled at the heat pouring off her as her nipples hardened further.

The soft, dark pink tips were elongated, stiff with her arousal and a tempting treat that spiked his already voracious appetite. His cock throbbed with the demand that he take her now, but his heart screamed out that he touch her first. He only wished the physical was what drove him. He longed to touch more than her soft breasts or her silken lips—he needed to touch her soul.

"You're so beautiful," he whispered as he lowered his head, smoothing his cheek over the curve of her breast until his lips raked the sensitive nipple. Her gasp of pleasure shook him.

"You're trying to tease me." She arched against him, her breathing rough and deep as he smoothed his hand along her trembling stomach to her parted thighs.

"Just trying?" he whispered as his lips smoothed over the satin delicacy of her breast. "I thought you could recognize clear intent when you saw it, sweetheart."

Her soft laughter was more a gasp as his tongue licked over her nipple. His hand smoothed to her inner thigh, coming close but never touching the syrupy-slick mound between her thighs.

"I want to taste every inch of you." His lips kissed over her breast, up her collarbone. "You're so sweet, so delicate and so damned hot you nearly burn me alive."

"What do you think you do to me?" Her voice was rough, husky from the pleasure he knew was moving through her.

"Let's get hotter," he growled an instant before his lips covered hers again.

Moans and hot little cries escaped their throats as Kane moved her to her back, coming over her, glorying in her touch. She no longer just accepted his lust, his hunger, she battled with it, met it, matched it. Her hands roved over his shoulders, her nails biting into his skin as he moaned at the pleasure. His lips caressed her jaw, her cheek, smoothing over the fine skin as his fingers moved between her thighs.

She was wet and hot for him, the sensitive folds of flesh parting easily as his fingers slid between them. Her hips rose, pressing her swollen clit into his fingers a second before he slid lower, testing the honeyed entrance to her vagina before moving back and circling her straining clit once again.

Sherra's hands gripped his shoulders, her neck arched, perspiration dewing her body as she rubbed against him. He closed his eyes at the pleasure of feeling her breasts stroking over his chest as she rubbed against him, her hands moving over his shoulders, her body undulating beneath him.

He fought to keep his movements slow and easy, to soothe even as he aroused her, to make her aware of every cell in her body reaching out to him. He could feel her now. In each caress of her hands over his back, the arch of her against him, the way she rubbed against him like the little cat she was. He could feel her acceptance clear to his soul.

His lips tracked every soft inch of her face, her neck, her breasts, watching as her skin flushed, her breathing becoming ragged before he moved lower.

Kane spread her thighs slowly, staring in wonder at the light pink and cream of her flesh there. Breeds were hairless on their genitals, and he had never seen anything as arousing as the silken lips of her pussy parted for him, the darker blush of the inner flesh, a passion fruit he had been addicted to since the first taste.

He stretched out between her spread thighs, staring up at her as he gave her a wicked smile. "My midnight snack — hot, wet kitty."

She blushed deeper. Kane would have laughed in sheer delight if he weren't so aroused he had to fight for every second of control. His fingers slid over the thick layer of juices that gathered there. Like warm syrup, it clung to his fingers and sensitized the tips.

"I'm not going to be able to stand this," she warned him weakly as her hands fell to the bed, clenching the blanket beneath her.

"Then we'll go insane together," he growled, reaching out to grip her fist and unlock her fingers from the material.

Watching her closely, he moved her hand to her breast, seeing the surprise that filled her gaze.

"Touch your breasts," he ordered huskily. "I want to watch your fingers playing with your nipples. I want to hear your pleasure, your excitement, Sherra. Give me that much, at least."

Her hands cupped the smooth globes of her breasts, her fingers moving to her hard nipples as his cock jerked at the erotic sight.

Watching her, his gaze going from her self-exploration to her darkening eyes, he lowered his head.

She jerked, a whimper escaping her lips as his tongue swiped through the glistening cream that lay heavy on her swollen cunt. She tasted like midnight and dreams, he thought. Elusive and ever-changing. He hummed his appreciation, his hands holding her thighs wide, his thumbs further parting the plump lips as he settled down for a feast of the senses.

He licked and lapped, circled her little clit and sucked at it strongly as her cries began to rise in volume. Her hips twisted, writhed beneath the pleasure, and soon he was tightening in his own raging need as he heard her crying out his name, begging for her release.

He moved lower, his tongue plunging into the velvet recess of her vagina as her cries escalated. Her knees were bent now, thighs spread wide, her hands on his head as she held him to her, her hips undulating, pressing her pussy against his devouring mouth as she fought for her orgasm.

"Not yet," he growled as he felt her shudder, sensing her nearing release.

He forced himself to his knees as she cried out her objection, gripping her wrists and pulling her into a sitting position.

"Shit!" His back arched as her lips attacked his flat abdomen, her tongue stroking, licking, as her hands gripped the tensed muscles of his buttocks.

Like the hungry cat he knew she could be, she devoured him in turn. He stared down at her, watching as her hands wrapped around his erection, her lips opening, her mouth enclosing the engorged, violently sensitive head of his cock.

"Sherra." His hand tangled in her hair as he shook his head desperately, fighting to hold onto his own control.

"Give me." She moved back to lick the crest of his erection as she spoke. "Fill my mouth, Kane. Let me taste all of you."

Her voice was thick, dazed, as she nearly swallowed him on the next stroke. Kane felt his shaft sink into her mouth, the head butting her throat for less than a second and stealing all his intentions to hold back.

"Then take it, baby." His hands tightened in her hair. "Take all of me."

It was like no other time that they had ever come together. It was hotter, sweeter, more intense than anything he could have imagined as he watched her suck his cock with greedy, slippery abandon.

Her eyes were drowsy, heavy-lidded, but she stared up at him, her lips enclosing the width of his tool as he thrust inside her with firm, shallow strokes and allowed her to choose the depth that she took him to.

It was paradise.

His balls tightened as her hands pumped the column of flesh, drawing his seed from his loins despite his best attempts to hold back his release.

"Baby, I'm going to come." He couldn't hold back, he couldn't deny the ecstasy for even a moment longer.

She hummed in agreement, her suckling strokes increasing as he felt a tingle at the base of his spine a second before it surged up his back in a brilliant jolt of electrical energy.

He stiffened, his lips pulling back from his teeth as his head arched back and he gave her every drop of semen boiling in his balls. It spurted from his cock to her rapidly swallowing throat as he groaned like a man possessed and gave himself over to the primal mating act they were now involved in.

When she had sucked the last drop of seed from the throbbing flesh, he pulled back, staring down at her heatedly a second before he pressed her to the bed and moved quickly between her thighs.

Her legs circled his hips as he pressed the engorged head of his cock at the entrance to her pussy. She was hot, her liquid heat trickled around the flared crest, making him shudder with the need to plunge home. He eased inside her instead.

Sherra fought the raging tempest growing inside her. Her entire body was sensitized, demanding his touch as she stared back at him, feeling the thick wedge of his cock stretching her. She watched as his hand lifted, his fingers moving to her cheek, touching her gently as she moaned out her need.

He had pushed her past a limit she didn't know she possessed. He had terrified her when he walked away from her, had torn at the rough scars covering her soul with his bleak sadness when she first came into the room. He had endured hell for her, just as she had because of him. She wasn't willing to hurt any longer, nor was she willing to do without her heart. Her Kane.

His fingertips touched her cheek as he slid home, stretching her, filling her. Her chest tightened with emotion, her skin heating at each point that their bodies connected.

"I would give my life for you," he whispered as his fingertips lifted and his thumb brushed over her cheek before moving to rest at her jawline.

Sherra whimpered. The emotion that pulsed in his voice was impossible to deny.

"No," she whispered, her hand covering his as her hips arched, the muscles of her pussy contracting around his erection. "Don't do that, Kane. Don't leave me again. I couldn't bear it…" Her breath hitched as tears filled her eyes. "I love you. I love you too much to ever live without you again."

He stilled. His blue eyes darkened with emotion, with a ravaging hunger as he came over her, one hand gripping her hips, the other her hair.

"You can't take it back again," he growled. "I won't let you."

Her short laugh was a sound between pleasure and agony. "I never took it back the first time. It was always yours, Kane. Always…"

His control disintegrated. In that second, the man fell away, the teasing, the tempting, were at an end.

Hard, driving strokes had her eyes widening as pleasure tore through her in ways it never had before. He was a demon, a sexual animal intent on possessing every part of her now. He couldn't go deep enough, hard enough. Both hands held her hips still as his lips buried at her neck, his breathing raspy, the intensity of his arousal driving them both now.

"Harder!" she screamed, though she feared harder would tear her asunder.

She couldn't get enough of him, couldn't ease the terrible buildup in her womb fast enough as he stroked the tissues of her vagina, stretching her, filling her until she wondered if she would survive it.

Kane's hips jackhammered his cock into her pussy, penetrating her violently as she screamed for more. They were fighting to breathe, her nails clawed at his back, her teeth bit deep into the mark on his chest as his locked onto her shoulder and they exploded.

Even death couldn't touch the complete oblivion that swept over them. Sherra swore she felt their souls merge as his cock slammed into the mouth of her womb and deep, strong spurts of his semen began to blast inside her.

Her womb contracted, convulsed, sucking greedily at the life-giving seed that spilled into it, even as Sherra locked her legs and arms around his body and surrendered to the orgasmic death that washed over them.

Chapter Fifteen

He was sleeping. Sherra lay draped over Kane's chest, exhausted, unwilling to move, yet unable to sleep. She could feel the imprint of the scars on his chest, hear his heart beating beneath her ear and fought the swirling, twisting emotions that began to churn inside her chest.

Hold it back, she ordered herself fiercely. *It's over. It's been over. There's no sense in dredging the past back up.* She had buried it in the deepest reaches of her mind years ago in order to survive. Now wasn't the time to drag it back out.

Kane shifted beneath her. His hands smoothed up her back, his head turning so he could bury his face in her hair.

"Mmm. Love you," he muttered as his arms contracted around her and the band around her heart tightened.

He was so fierce, so hard and yet a part of him was so filled with confidence that his love alone could heal the wounds on her soul, the demons in her mind. Perhaps, over the months, he had in part eased that pain, but there was still so much more left inside her.

Kane, help me! She flinched as the memory of her own screams echoed through her mind.

Her stomach clenched, razor-sharp pain streaking through her womb at the memory of that blinding moment she had realized she was losing the child he had given her.

She wanted to get up then. Wanted to rush from the room and hide from the memories as she always had. She needed to escape, but something more powerful held her where she was. Held her locked tight in Kane's arms while everything inside her mind rejected the memories and the emotions that being there caused.

It wasn't meant to be, Sherra. Dayan's voice was a demonic resonation from the past. *It was an abomination. There was no humanity in it...*

She flinched as she remembered the words. Doc Martin had told her differently years later, of course, that the development of the fetus had been perfectly normal. But then, horror had singed her.

I saw him leave, Sherra. Escaping to save his own skin. He won't be back. She had screamed Kane's name as Dayan was forced to hold her down while the scientists and doctors attempted to save her life. But there had been no saving the baby that had barely begun.

She didn't want to remember. She closed her eyes, trying to hold back the tears as the memories began to rip through her. Violent, filled with her screams, demonic laughter and images that she had hidden from herself for so long.

The guards had raped her less than a month after her miscarriage. The drugs that had been forced into her body had mercifully dulled the memories, but nothing could dull the knowledge.

She could hear their laughter in her nightmares.

"Take it, bitch. You can fuck that bastard Kane, you can fuck us..."

No! Despite her exhaustion she attempted to jump away from the man holding her, to escape the nightmarish visuals playing out inside her head.

"Sherra." His arms tightened around her, his lips pressing to her forehead. "You can't keep running, baby. You have to stop. Now."

"Let me go." She realized then that tears wet her cheeks, dripped to her breasts. Sobs were ripping inside her chest as she fought to hold them back.

"I can't let you go." The sound of his voice had her staring down at him as she jerked back.

Shock held her still for a long moment before her hand reached out, her fingers touching the moisture on his cheeks.

"Don't," she whimpered, shaking as her own tears fell faster. "Oh God, Kane, don't let me do this."

"It was my baby, too." His voice was husky, filled with regret, with pain. "But even more than that, Sherra, you're my soul. You're every breath I take. I would give my life to have saved you. I would give it now if it would mean I could go back and spare you this pain." The dampness from his eyes soaked the swarthy complexion, lined with pain and regret. "I would do anything, everything, baby, to ease this pain for you."

She was shuddering with her sobs now, fighting to hold them back, to keep the pain inside, buried, where it could never hurt her again.

"I wanted to die," she suddenly wailed, feeling him flinch, seeing the pain that tightened his face and made his own tears run faster. "I begged them to kill me." He rolled her to the bed, his arms wrapping tightly around her, sheltering her, holding her steady as her soul collapsed and her sobs echoed around them. "I begged them to let me die because I couldn't face it... I couldn't survive without you..." She was beating at his chest, her blows weak and ineffectual as the years of resounding agony poured free. "I wanted to die without you... And now, I don't know how to accept that you're here... I don't know how to live..."

"It's okay, baby." He rocked her, soothed her. Against his scarred chest he allowed her to shed the tears that she had held back for so many years. "One day at a time, Sherra," he told her huskily. "We'll both learn to live again, one day at a time..."

The heart that had shattered within Kane's chest so many years ago broke again. The temporary patches he had effected to survive ripped apart, leaving his soul bleeding as he held his woman in his arms and shared her agonized tears. The child he had never known had been taken from him, but the woman he had loved beyond life had been scarred in a way that had never healed, would never truly heal.

"I would dream of you," he finally whispered, clearing his throat as he tried to talk through the emotions tearing him apart. "After they told me you were dead, I would dream of you. Dream of rescuing you, holding you. I would dream of what could have been, what should have been. When I awoke, the pain would nearly destroy me, because it was only a dream. But it's not a dream now, baby. I'm here with you. I'm holding you. And God help me, if I have to let you go again, it will kill me."

Her breath hitched.

"I didn't want to love you," she whispered. "But when I saw you again for the first time, I knew I had never stopped." She shook her head, weariness filling her voice. "I never stopped, Kane. No matter how hard I tried."

"I won't let you go, Sherra. Not ever again." He held on tighter to her, flipping the blanket over her when she shivered, cocooning her with his warmth. "Just hold onto me, baby. I'm right here. I'll always be here."

He felt her slip into an exhausted sleep then. Her body slowly relaxed in his arms, her head resting comfortably against his shoulder as he allowed himself to hope, to pray that the wounds would finally begin to close.

"I love you, kitten," he whispered as his own eyes closed and sleep took him. A gentle, healing sleep, free of pain or demons, and for once without the haunting arousal that had taunted him for so many years.

* * * * *

Sherra awoke to a sweet languor that she couldn't remember having ever known. Even after that first night with Kane she hadn't know this sense of satiation, of complete contentment. His arms, strong and warm, had enfolded her throughout the night, the sound of his heartbeat echoing at her ear had comforted her, soothed her.

There had been no nightmares, there had been no demons rising from the twisted half memories that had snaked through her unconsciousness on even the best of nights. There had been none in Kane's arms.

"Awake?" His voice was drowsy, rough and sexy. It sent a small tremor of awareness skating up her spine and heat spearing between her thighs.

"Awake." She smiled, her tongue licking lazily at the reddened mark on his chest.

It was sensitive. She felt the shudder of response that tightened his muscles, saw the tenting of the sheet as his cock began to harden.

She lifted the light cover, peeking under it with false curiosity and then with heated wonder.

Had she ever taken the time to really *look* at Kane's cock?

She flipped the sheet off his body, moving down until her head rested on his tight abs and she watched the slow engorging of all that luscious meat. Her mouth watered at the sight of the dark, heavily veined shaft and the wide flared head that grew faintly damp with the pearly drops of pre-come that seeped from its slitted eye.

She ran her hand along the side of his leg, then over the lightly haired thigh to the heavy weight of his scrotum. She cupped the silky flesh in her palm, watching as the bulbous head of his cock pulsed until it spilled yet another drop of its creamy fluid.

"Sherra, baby." There was a thread of laughter in his voice. "It's not nice to tease a horny man."

"Tease?" Her tongue licked over the indention of his belly button as the little droplet spilled to his hard stomach. "Am I teasing?"

She blew a soft breath over the sensitive crest and watched as it flexed again, swelling further in response to the warm air blowing over it. In response to her. Amazement filled her. The first time she had seen him, so many years ago, he had filled her with a sense of wonder and excitement. All other males paled in comparison to Kane. And still, there was no other man that she could even consider doing this with.

"Sherra, kitten," he growled. "Are you going to do anything with that hard-on you've brought to life or are you going to admire it all day?"

"It's well worth admiring," she whispered as she felt his scrotum tighten, watched the beat of his blood in the ridge of veins that extended around the thick flesh. "It's actually a sight to make a grown woman's mouth water at the thought of tasting it," she assured him with a smile as the heavy cock jerked in reflex at her words.

"Just the thought?" he asked her, his voice strained as the hard muscles of his abdomen tightened beneath her head.

"Well, the intention?" she asked as her tongue flicked out that last small distance and swiped over the throbbing head of his erection.

Kane gasped, his hands tightening in her hair as he lifted his hips, pressing his cock firmly against her lips. Sherra opened wide, her tongue licking greedily around the flared crest as her mouth sucked him in. His groan was a dark, rough growl of passion and need that sent her own pulse rate rocketing and her pussy flaming.

She clenched her thighs to relieve the pressure, a moan slipping past her throat as she tasted more of the salty seed that spilled into her mouth.

"Come here." Kane's order was harsh, the words dragged from his chest as his hand lowered to her hip. "Come over me, baby, let me taste that sweet kitty."

Fiery waves of lust seared her womb as she lifted to her knees, her mouth lowering to take more of his erection as he guided her until her thighs bracketed his face.

The first touch of his tongue caused her to flinch with the pleasure. A second later she pressed her pussy closer, eager for more, desperate to feel his tongue plunging deep inside the hungry depths of her cunt.

Her mouth lowered on the flesh rising hard and eager from between his thighs, trying to swallow as much of the thick shaft as possible. The steady, greedy licks of his tongue and the suction of his lips on her pussy as he drove her insane was all she needed to lose what little sanity she still possessed as she tried to consume his cock.

She wanted all of him, his semen filling her mouth, spilling down her throat as he sucked every drop of cream from her pussy. She wanted it now. Needed him now.

The sounds of heated moans and hungry suckling mouths wrapped around her. Her fingers cupped and caressed his balls as his lips surrounded her clit and two fingers pushed demandingly inside her vagina. She jerked, driving herself harder on the penetration as she took his cock deeper, sucking it eagerly as his mouth ate with greedy ferocity at her creamy cunt.

Her orgasm was building. She could feel it tightening in her womb even as she felt Kane's scrotum drawing up tight to the base of his erection as her other hand pumped the hard length of his shaft. She wanted to taste him. Wanted to feel every hot drop of his seed shooting into her throat.

She felt his fingers thrusting into her harder, deeper, a second before he withdrew, drawing her juices back to the entrance of her anus before pushing them deep inside her pussy once again, joining them with a firm, heated stroke of a finger up her ass.

Sherra tightened, a scream escaping her throat, vibrating around his cock as she exploded. At the moment of her release, Kane groaned hard and deep, his fingers quickening inside her, his tongue lashing at her throbbing clit as his hips thrust upward, burying his cock deeper in her mouth as his come began to pulse in fast, hard jets from the tip of his cock.

He filled her mouth, the taste driving her higher as she swallowed every rich drop, her moans a plea for more.

"Enough." He lifted her away from him, pushing her to the bed when she struggled against him, her hands pressing him back to the mattress.

"No. Like this." She rose above him, throwing her thigh over his hips, rubbing the wet flesh of her cunt over the hard ridge of his erection before allowing the wide head to tuck against the entrance to her pussy.

"Hard, Kane," she whispered, lowering her lips to his as she prepared for the invasion. "Hard…"

Her back bowed, her wail of satisfaction and pleasure piercing the silence of the room as he impaled her, separating the gripping tissues with one fierce, determined thrust.

There was no struggle for control, no attempts to delay the driving need for orgasm. The sounds of wet flesh slapping together, whispered, hungry growls and heated cries filled the air around them.

Sherra lowered her head to his chest, her tongue licking over the mark she had given him a second before she scraped it with her lethal canines and applied a firm, erotic suction to the overly sensitive flesh.

His release triggered hers. Hard, convulsive, it ripped through them, tying them together, binding them, and once and for all piercing the final barriers to Sherra's soul.

"I love you," Kane cried out as he jerked beneath her, filling her with his seed, his hands hard on her hips as he held her to him. "God help me, Sherra, I love you…"

Her head raised, a languorous satiation spreading through her body, leaving her drowsy, weak, and yet filled with a strength she hadn't known she possessed.

Her hand reached out, her fingertips caressing his cheek as his surprise at the touch filled his eyes. And Sherra knew in that moment, if she ever lost him again she wouldn't, *couldn't* survive the pain.

* * * * *

"I'd like you to move your things into my room." Kane made the surprise announcement as they were gearing up for the day.

Dressed in her customary snug black pants and matching tank top with her hair braided down her back, Sherra was pulling on her jacket when he spoke. She paused before shrugging the material farther up her shoulders and carefully checking the weapon holstered on her thigh.

"Did you hear me, Sherra?" She could feel the determination emanating from him and hid her smile at the sound.

"I hear you." She cleared her throat lightly. "I can take care of that this evening after I meet with Doc."

Silence descended behind her, a thick anticipatory silence that throbbed like a silent heartbeat. It could be felt, but it couldn't be heard with anything more than the internal senses.

"I won't let you go. Ever," he told her then, moving behind her, his arms coming around her waist as she allowed her head to fall back to his shoulder.

"I haven't asked you to," she said. "I'm stubborn, Kane. I'm not stupid."

It wasn't easy for her, letting go of the pain and dealing with the fears that still haunted her. But she knew she hadn't truly been living until Kane reappeared in her life. She had been existing, nothing more. She didn't want to exist any longer. She needed to live, she needed to love.

"Very stubborn," he amended, kissing the side of her neck softly.

Sherra smiled, a wry curve of her lips as she acknowledged the statement.

"It won't be easy," she finally whispered. "*I* won't be easy. There are still scars," she warned him.

His arms tightened around her. "We'll heal them together, Sherra. However we need to."

She nodded slowly before standing straight again. "Time to go to work, stud," she said softly, her voice filled with amusement. "You can play later."

"Sounds good to me," he chuckled as he released her. "I'm heading to the guesthouse with Callan and Taber this morning. Lawrence has proposed an idea that could work to get the houses we need in place faster, combining both our ideas," he said, more than a little amused. "Lawrence Industries has a small construction sideline headed by one of his most trusted friends. He's willing to provide the materials at a cut-rate cost as well as technical assistance in training our men to build what they need themselves," he told her. "We have enough land here to make them self-sufficient to a degree, and I still feel that's the best way to go."

Sherra sighed in resignation. Unfortunately, she agreed with him, but they needed buildings now, not months down the road. Perhaps this could be the solution to it.

"Let me know how it goes." She finally nodded in agreement. "I have to do another inventory check today. Somehow the count on the rifles Merc insisted we buy is off by one. I have to figure out if it's our mistake or the supplier's. I hate it when weapons are off, Kane. It makes me paranoid."

"No kidding. Let me know what you find out. We've not had any non-secured personnel other than the Lawrences, and security on them has been too tight to allow for a theft that far away from their guesthouse, but we need it solved." He grimaced as he pulled on a light jacket over his dark blue cotton shirt. "I'll get hold of you later and see if we can't meet for a little…uhh, lunch." He wagged his eyebrows at her as he grinned wickedly. "Later, kitten." He kissed her lightly on the forehead before leaving the room and heading down the hallway.

Sherra stood still, aware of the silly little smile on her face as Kane left. There had been no choice left last night but to trust him, to give him everything blooming within her. Not just the hunger for his cock, but the hunger for his touch, his smile, his laughter. A chance to heal.

"Damn man. I can't understand him, and Merinus won't let me kill him," she drawled in amusement as she shook her head and moved for the door. She might as well just give in and love him, she finally told herself as she headed to her own room. And why wait to begin moving into the life he was offering her?

* * * * *

"Sherra?" The little voice and the soft knock at her door had Sherra stiffening in reaction as she recognized Cassie's voice.

The door opened slowly and the little girl peeked in. Her face was somber, her long dark hair laying in thick curls down her back as she stepped into the bedroom.

"Who's watching you today, Cassie?" Sherra asked curiously.

"I don't know, Sherra." The little girl was confused. "I woke up and no one was there. Someone is always there when I wake up."

Sherra stared at the little girl with a frown. Cassie still wore her gown and robe and clutched her teddy bear like a lifeline.

"I'm scared, Sherra," she whispered. "My fairy said to come up here. She seems kinda worried." The little girl moved closer as though in need of comfort or protection.

Sherra grabbed her communications link from the dresser and pulled it on over her head as she switched it to the main channel. She knew Taber, Callan, Kane and Dawn were with the Lawrences, but they wouldn't have left the little girl without a guard.

"Who has house duty?" she snapped into the link.

No one answered.

"Cassie, did you see anyone when you came up here?" Sherra asked her quietly, moving to the French doors and peeking past the curtains to the yard outside.

"No." Cassie was holding her teddy bear closer now. "I didn't see anyone, Sherra."

"Do you know how to hide, Cassie?" Sherra asked her, feeling the familiar rise of danger edging up her spine.

Cassie's eyes widened in sudden fear. Her lower lip trembled. "I want my momma," she suddenly whispered, a breath of sound that showed the little girl knew well the dangers that could be moving outside their room. "Momma doesn't leave me alone."

Shit. No one was moving outside. Where the hell were the guards?

"Okay." Sherra turned back to the little girl. "Do you know how to be quiet? No matter what?"

Cassie nodded fiercely.

"I want you to stay right behind me, Cassie. And don't say a word. Don't make a sound unless I tell you to. We're going to go to Merinus' room. Okay?"

Cassie nodded quickly.

Moving to the door, Sherra pulled the gun free of her holster and peeked out carefully. All the doors were closed, the guard normally on duty at the end of the hall absent. Damn. Damn.

She glanced behind her at the kid. She was pale, trembling and moving with damned near every shift of Sherra's body.

"Okay, nice and quiet," Sherra whispered as she eased the door open.

She stepped out into the hallway, checked it quickly then pulled Cassie from the bedroom and moved stealthily for the second wing of the upstairs bedrooms where Callan and Merinus' suite was located. Pausing at the turn in the hall, she flattened Cassie against the wall then checked it as well. No one. Fuck. Where the hell were they?

Moving carefully down the carpeted hall, her senses razor-sharp, she moved for Merinus' room. She was no more than three doors from it when the new scent slammed into her head. Alien. Foreign. Waiting on them.

She stopped. There were two doors between her and Merinus' room and one of them could possibly be opened just enough to allow anyone hiding in the room to see her pass by.

Sherra moved for the door beside her. Turning the knob she eased it open and pressed Cassie inside before following her. Closing it just as silently, she indicated silence to the little girl as she moved to the wide window on the other side of the room.

Looking out, she breathed a sigh of relief as she caught sight of two guards moving along the perimeters of the house grounds. Opening the curtains wide she slowly lifted the window, praying she wasn't giving her position away to the enemy two doors down.

She was within a second of gaining their attention when she saw them go down. First one, then the other. Her eyes widened. No sound was made, but within a second they had fallen, dead or unconscious, she wasn't certain.

Fuck. Fuck. Looking around frantically she dragged Cassie to the closet on the other side of the room.

"You stay here." She pushed the tearful child into the small room. "I mean it, Cassie. No one will know but me where you are hidden. You don't move. Do you hear me?"

She kept her lips at Cassie's ear, her heart breaking as the little girl shook and shuddered, though she nodded her head quickly.

"Stay," she ordered her again before backing away and closing the door slowly.

Whoever was waiting in the room up the hall had somehow managed to take out the communications link and/or the communications personnel and was quietly waiting. For what?

She moved back to the door and opened it slowly, peering down the hall but seeing nothing that would immediately raise her suspicions. She stepped from the room, flattening herself against the wall, weapon held ready, watching intently.

A second later Merinus' doorknob turned. Aiming her weapon, Sherra watched coldly as it opened and the other woman stood framed in the doorway, shock widening her eyes at the gun Sherra had leveled at her. Just as quickly, the door closed, then locked.

Smart. Sherra smiled with cold determination. At least the other woman was safe. That was all that mattered. She could almost feel the waves of fury pouring from the other room now. Whoever was in there had seen Merinus' escape back into her room as well.

A second later three loud reports sounded from Merinus' room. The gunshots were a clear signal to any Breed within hearing distance. The bastard might have taken out the guards in the house, and those on the grounds, but there was no way he could have gotten them all.

She heard a curse, soft, filled with menace, and aimed her gun at the approximate height to severely wound rather than kill. There was only two ways out of that room, the window or the door. But she wasn't expecting what stepped from the room.

Roni came first, closely followed by the chauffeur/nurse who had come in with the Lawrences several days before. There was a smug victorious smile on the man's face as he held the gun to Roni's temple and kept her carefully in front of him.

"Very lucky," he grunted. "But not quite good enough."

He faced Sherra with malicious contempt.

"So where's the kid? She wasn't in her room or with her guard."

Sherra kept her expression cold and her gun ready. "If I knew, I wouldn't tell you."

His beady eyes glittered with fury. "Drop the gun or I'll kill her."

Sherra shook her head as she allowed a mocking smile to curl her lips. "No way. And if you kill her, you'll fall in the next second."

He wasn't nervous. He was cold, calculating. He had Roni by the hair, a tenuous grip at best, his gun at her temple. Sherra's eyes met Roni's. She could see the resignation in the other woman's eyes. Somehow he had taken out their men. Sherra wasn't certain how he could have managed to do it, but he had.

"Well, we could consider it a standoff." He smiled slowly, like a viper preparing to strike. "You think that warning is going to get help here in time? I made sure your boys were out for several more hours. The best." He grunted sarcastically. "They were easy, Sherra."

Sherra shrugged lightly. "Seems you forgot about me, though. I'm not so easy."

Her gaze met Roni's. The other woman moved her eyes up to indicate the hand holding her hair, then quickly looked to the floor. God, could she pull it off? She did it again, frantically. Up, then down. Was she going to drop?

Sherra angled her weapon at Roni's head. If the other woman didn't move fast enough… She swallowed tightly.

Suddenly, Roni dropped. His gun went off the same second Sherra's did. The bullet dropped the would-be assassin immediately as she ran to him, kicking the gun aside before dropping beside Roni.

"Bastard!" Roni came up like a demon, lips curled back, fury lighting her eyes as she kicked the fallen would-be assassin.

Merinus' door flew open at the same time feet pounded on the stairs and male voices began to scream out in fury. It was chaos.

Kane, Callan, Taber, more than a dozen Feline guards and Seth Lawrence rushed into the hallway.

"Are you happy now, Mr. Lawrence?" Sherra snarled in his face as Taber rushed for his wife. "Was it worth it?"

He stared down at the chauffeur, his gaze somber, filled with misery before it went to his sister. Regret flickered in his eyes.

"No, Miss Callahan, it wasn't." But he didn't take his eyes off his sister.

"Sherra, you didn't kill him," Kane said in surprise as he stood up from the fallen body. "Flesh wound."

"Not yet," she snapped as she turned back to him. "I want to know who hired him first. Then I'll kill him." She stared back at Kane with brutal fury. "This time, Breed Law will be enforced."

She turned and marched back to the room where Cassie awaited her. Pulling the closet door open she knelt in front of the sobbing girl, her heart clenching. Cassie didn't make a sound, but her shoulders were shaking violently as she held her teddy bear close to her.

"Come on, Cassie. It's all over now," Sherra whispered as she picked her up.

"I want my momma." The heartrending sobs came then. "I want my momma now. Now. If you don't get my momma I'm gonna bite all of you. I will. I will…" She buried her head in Sherra's shoulder, her arms wrapping tightly around her as her sobs tore through the room.

Sherra turned back to Kane, tears filling her own eyes as he watched her with quiet pain.

"Come here, Cassie." Callan moved to Sherra's side, his wife staying close beside him as he eased the little girl from his sister's arms.

She went easily, and though her tears didn't abate, neither did her demands for her momma. Kane lifted Sherra in his arms and only then did she realize that she was shaking, hard shudders of reaction, fury and fear quaking through her.

Sherra wrapped her arms around his shoulders, burying her face against his neck as she let the tears free. She cried for the past, the betrayals, the losses, the child they had never known. The bitterness flowed from her in deep, gulping sobs as she held onto him. Her support, her heart.

Chapter Sixteen

The Terrible Tylers converged on the property within hours. Six brothers, along with their father, John Tyler, and their uncle, Senator Samuel Tyler. It was pandemonium and Sherra completely understood why Merinus was always so reluctant to have them all at the estate at the same time. The next morning, after her required visit to see Doc Martin, Sherra understood why.

They were hardheaded, stubborn and opinionated. Every one of them had their own idea of how things should be handled and every discussion turned into a war of words. But they all loved Merinus, and they were all determined they were now there for the duration to be certain she was protected.

"This isn't good, Sherra," Tanner commented from beside her as they both stood in the doorway of the spacious formal dining room and watched the debates rage with a sense of growing horror. "They'll end up killing each other."

Sherra snorted absently. "It could save us the trouble."

Tanner chuckled at that, the amusement in the sound causing her lips to curve as well.

"Watch how they hover over Merinus and Roni." He nodded to the group of men, including Callan and Taber.

Merinus looked as though she were in mortal pain as she attempted to come to her feet. Immediately, at least half a dozen of the men jumped to help her. Thinking they were otherwise occupied, Roni attempted to escape. They weren't having that, either. For the time being, the two women were trapped in the middle of testosterone protective hell. Thankfully, Kane had listened when Sherra had bared her teeth and snarled that she would kill the first man who attempted to "protect" her.

"Those poor women," she breathed out roughly.

Tanner turned his gaze on her then. His oddly striped black hair fell over his brow, the gold strands that grew through it matched the amber color of his eyes. They were an odd, eerie amber, almost glowing in his darkly tanned face.

He had worn contacts and colored his hair while they were in hiding, so Sherra was used to seeing a much more toned-down version of her brother. Now, he did nothing to hide who he was, and did everything to make up for the years he had been forced to conceal his true nature.

"So when are you going to tell Kane you're pregnant?" He shocked her with the question, keeping his voice low so that only she heard, but the laughter in his voice made her want to hit him.

Sherra stiffened. She had only learned the truth herself an hour before, during the exam Kane had ordered after they had dragged the assassin off to a holding cell. Thankfully, her mate had been busy securing the estate and hadn't been with her during the visit.

Doc Martin was as confused by the pregnancy as Sherra was. According to him, somehow the hormone raging through her body had begun to repair the break in her fallopian tubes and heal the surgery he had performed years before in preparation for the fertilization of her womb.

He had scratched his head and mumbled vague phrases that made little sense to her other than the fact that Breeds were enigmas and he needed more help.

"No answer?" Tanner smirked when she stayed silent.

"Shut up, Tanner," she growled. "Give me a chance to get used to it myself."

She couldn't believe it. It was more than she had ever prayed for. She winced as she watched the two women in the dining room fighting to breathe as the men fought around them, discussing their protection and ignoring their attempts to escape them. She prayed that wasn't a glimpse of her own pregnancy in the coming months. They would make her crazy.

"Tell them." He nodded into the room with a chuckle. "They'll help you get used to it."

She was starting to regret his return. His helicopter had landed just ahead of the Tylers', carrying him, Merc and Simon Quatres. Cassie had been loaded quickly into the machine to rush her to her wounded mother's side. Dash and Elizabeth had completed their mission, stilling the most dangerous threat to Cassie's life. The small family would go into hiding after Elizabeth's recovery though, Tanner had reported. Cassie, and now the child Elizabeth was carrying as well, would all be in danger until the world came to grips with the new species now inhabiting it. And it didn't look like that was going to happen anytime soon.

"Tanner, go find someone else to torture and torment," Sherra finally ordered him as her gaze caught Kane's and she looked upstairs slowly.

She needed to share the news with him, to see his face when she told him he was going to be a father. To exorcise the ghosts of the past.

As Kane turned to his father, a sudden shrill whistle pierced the room. All eyes turned to Merinus, widening in surprise as she stared at them in fury.

"Enough, dammit!" she yelled out to the room of men as Roni jumped to her feet and pushed Taber's hand aside so she could move to the other woman's side. "We're pregnant, not wounded and definitely not in any way incapacitated. Get over the he-man crap now."

A stunned silence filled the room as she punctuated her words with a hard smack to the back of her youngest brother Gray's head when he started to argue. It wasn't a small sisterly pat.

"Now." Merinus adjusted the shoulders of her maternity smock as she gave them all a narrow-eyed look. "I'm sick of all of you. I want a glass of milk, a pack of Oreos, and some peace. You can argue amongst yourselves all you want to, but Roni and I have had enough. We expect our milk and cookies in my room immediately."

The two women moved for the doorway when a set of twins rose to their feet as though to stop them.

"Sit back down, assholes," Merinus snarled. "Before I make good on my threat to shoot you all."

They sat down, though indulgent smiles crossed their faces.

"Better escape yourself, Sherra," Merinus muttered as Tanner stepped back to allow the women to pass. "You'll be next."

Sherra grunted, her hand caressing the butt of the weapon still strapped to her thigh. "I won't just threaten to shoot them," she muttered. "I will." She gave Kane a look of warning. She received a wicked, daring smile in return. A smile that sent her pulse rate rocketing and her pussy creaming in anticipation.

Merinus and Roni moved quickly past her and headed to the elevator at the far end of the entryway. Merinus was evidently playing it safe for the time being. As she turned back to Kane, Sherra wondered how he would handle attempting to protect her. Surprisingly enough, the thought of Kane hovering over her and their child didn't bother her so much. Those brothers of his would have to go, though.

"I say we adjourn this fight for the time being," Kane announced as Sherra once again indicated her desire to return to their room. "Caleb," he turned to one of the twins, "you and Seth get everyone together and get the plans for those houses started. Uncle Sam, you do something with that Breed Liaison in D.C. I want dependable satellite intel on those caves. Dad, you can get with Merinus later about the report she's preparing, we want worldwide coverage on this. It has to stop."

His voice hardened on the last words, his gaze turning cold as his fury seeped to the surface. The assassin had come much too close to the sister they all treasured. They wouldn't allow it to happen again.

As Kane strode toward her, Sherra felt a warmth and security infuse her entire being. He was hers. Finally. Completely. Her hand moved to her abdomen, her fingers spreading across it as the truth finally hit her. Their child rested there. Their baby. The joy that bloomed in her heart spread throughout her body as her lips curved into a smile she couldn't contain.

Kane stopped several feet from her, seeing the joy, the utter complete happiness that suffused her face and seemed to light up the room around her. She seemed to glow, to give a heat and radiant light that took him aback. Her eyes seemed greener, her soft skin creamier, while at the same time she seemed more mysterious and in contradiction, more touchable than ever before. His gaze went over her. What was different?

Then his eyes paused at her abdomen, the way her hand lay over it, her fingers splayed as though in protection and amazement. He felt his heart race, his mouth go dry. The heat had been easing, he realized that now, where he hadn't before. There had been moments that he hadn't craved to be buried inside her. Not often, he admitted, but moments. And though the hunger was still there, it was more natural, softer.

He took another step toward her, distantly aware of the others behind him, the silence surrounding them. But all he could hear was his own heartbeat, all he could see was the knowledge glowing in Sherra's eyes. And it brought him to his knees. Literally.

"Kane." Her shocked exclamation didn't stop him as he clasped her hips and buried his face against her stomach.

He was overwhelmed. Emotion churned inside him, ripping through his chest, filling his heart. She was carrying his baby. He swore he could feel it beneath his cheek—life, a renewal to all the dreams they had once believed were lost to them.

"I love you." His arms wrapped around her as he laid a tender kiss on her abdomen. "God help me, Sherra, I love you."

"Kane, they're watching you," she whispered, but there was no shame in her voice, only laughter, only love.

"Let them." He moved back just enough to watch as he splayed his fingers over her flat stomach.

His fingers were trembling—hell, his whole body was trembling as he stared up at her, weakened by the emotion he saw in her gaze and the knowledge of the child growing in her body.

"How?" He shook his head. He had resigned himself to never healing that part of the past for either of them.

She reached out, her fingertips touching his face.

"Doc's not sure." She cleared her throat as she glanced back at the room full of men behind them. "Kane, if they start hovering over me, I'm going to shoot them."

"Ignore them." He shook his head as he came slowly to his feet. "You're sure?"

He couldn't stop touching her. Her hand rested on his shoulder now as his ran up her arm, caressing the soft skin, marveling at the miracle she was to his life.

"Well, Doc says it's so." She shrugged with a small grin. "What do you think?"

Kane glanced behind him then. His damned brothers were snickering, but that was okay, let them snicker, he had the world in his arms now.

He turned back to her with a grin and whispered, "I think we need to go check for ourselves, just to be certain."

Her laughter was a salve to his soul, a sound of joy and dreams and all the stubborn hopes he had carried with him for years.

"Definitely," she answered, turning to lead the way up the stairs.

Kane didn't give her time to take the first step. He picked her up in his arms instead.

"Dammit, Kane, I'll shoot you, too," she threatened fiercely as he started up the steps. "Put me down before you drop me."

"Not a chance," he promised, glancing down at her, loving that dark little frown on her face as he headed for their bedroom. "I'll never drop you, baby, and I'll never let you go. Never again, Sherra."

She touched his face and heat exploded inside him. A touch, given freely, a mate's caress, as he had come to call it when he saw it between Callan and Merinus.

"Never again, Kane," she agreed before she rested her head against his shoulder, her arms wrapping around his shoulders as she held onto him. "Never again."

Epilogue

Kane massaged his neck tiredly, the ache from the debilitating blow the day before still smarting. The blow to his pride was worse, though. When he had walked into the guesthouse, he just hadn't been prepared. Which was no excuse.

The guards had been outside the guesthouse, relaxed and comfortable. The chauffeur had been cordial as he opened the door. There had been no warning of what awaited him inside. A second later, blinding pain had rendered him unconscious. As unconscious as Callan, Taber and Dawn were.

The assassin hadn't wasted any time. The house guards had been systematically tranquilized, then bound hand and foot before he began to make his way to his victims. He had found Roni first, taking her with him. Cassie had left her room by then, foiling his attempts to get to her. As he made his way to Merinus' room he had heard something along the other hall that had sent him scurrying into that spare bedroom. Likely little Cassie's knock at Sherra's door.

The assassin had been hired by Aaron Lawrence to help kidnap his daughter. But he had been approached later by the Purist Society to kill her instead. He had used the elder Lawrence to gain his way into the compound and to carry out the plan the Society had laid out. A society backed by the remaining, secretive members of the Genetics Council. And he had almost succeeded.

"This has to stop." Callan stood at the window of the office, his shoulders thrown back, his long mane of hair held back by a leather strip at his nape. He looked just as wild as his nature. "One of these days, they'll succeed."

Kane ran his hands over his closely cropped hair in frustration as he stared at his quiet sister. Merinus had said little since coming into the meeting. She had been crying, though. Her eyes were red and swollen from those tears. Dawn was still in the medical facility downstairs. She had taken the brunt of the injuries. She had been the first one the assassin had attacked. After taking out the other two guards he had tortured both her and Seth Lawrence as he repeatedly hit her, threatening to rape her as he demanded the locations of the rooms inside.

"We enact Breed Law," Sherra snapped then. "We have it for a reason."

"If you enact the Law, you lose the majority of public support." The government advisor, Senator Samuel Tyler, Kane's uncle, watched them all sympathetically. "You'll also lose support within the government. Things could go from sugar to shit fast, Sherra."

"And it's not now?" She turned on the distinguished politician furiously. "That was your niece he nearly killed, Tyler. Would you have approved it if he succeeded?"

"I would have killed him myself," he snapped back, just as angry, his brown eyes darkening further as she confronted him. "I'm not telling you what to do, Sherra, I'm warning you that no matter who dies, that's what will happen. An act of aggression from the Breeds will only fuel those like the Purists further. In turn, the propaganda could destroy any chance of acceptance that you could have."

"Well, hell, let's just let them pick us and our children off one by one," she argued back at him. "You and your people let that pimply faced bastard who fired the missile at the house off no more than a week ago. The son of a bitch is already free and another takes his place. Where does it stop, Senator?"

"Enough, Sherra." Kane came tiredly to his feet, unwilling to see the danger they faced turning into a battle between the Breeds and the government. "This isn't the way to do it."

He wrapped his fingers around the nape of her neck, massaging the tense muscles there as she leaned into him comfortably. Her expression was tormented as his other hand covered her abdomen. Their child rested there. Another child in danger.

"We fight back." Callan's voice stilled them all.

"Callan, think about this…" Sam Tyler spoke up.

"Shut up, Sam," John Tyler, the patriarch of the family ordered coolly. "I know your stand. If you don't want to hear what's about to be said then go back to Washington. I'll be damned if I'll stand behind you on this one."

Kane turned back to his father. Surrounding Merinus were the Tyler brothers. All of them. The meeting room was nearly filled to capacity. Kane knew what was getting ready to come. He knew, because it was a suggestion he had made himself more than a month ago.

Callan moved back to the center of the room. "We strike back at the Purists and the Council members attempting to move against us."

"Strike back?" Sam was about to have another of his political seizures, Kane could see. Thankfully, he might be an uptight bastard, but when it came to his family, he was a loyal one.

"Merc will put together two teams," Callan said coldly. "They want to send in assassins? Let them see what happens when they're faced with the people trained to take out men like that on a daily basis. We were trained to track, hunt and kill. Tanner and Merinus, along with John and the paper, will keep propaganda in force. But our people will now enact Breed Law. Silently. Eventually, they'll get the message. No more calls will be made to Washington after an attack. No more pleas for justice. We'll take care of our own."

Sam gazed around at the men and women facing him. Kane could see the resignation, even the shuttered agreement in his gaze.

"Tell me what you need," he said then. "I'll make sure you get it."

"We'll turn this one over to you. It's too late to hide it," Callan said, his voice unemotional. "If he's freed by your so-called justice system, within a month, he will meet a very unfortunate end. From this day forward, we will make certain Breed affairs stay just that. Breed affairs."

"Don't get caught," Sam ordered roughly. "God help us all, Callan, if you get caught."

"God help us all, Senator, if this doesn't stop. I won't see more of my people die as I beg for justice. I refuse to allow this situation to continue. From here on out, we fight back."

* * * * *

Tanner entered the infirmary, his gaze going to the narrow bed that held the small form of his Pride sister and the man sitting silently beside her.

"Has she woken up yet?" He sat down in the spare chair on the other side of the bed.

Seth Lawrence breathed out deeply. "For a few minutes. She didn't say anything."

Tanner nodded. "They raped her in those labs," he said quietly as he stared at the unconscious woman. "No drugs, nothing. She was the runt and they enjoyed hurting her."

He watched the rage fill Lawrence's eyes.

"I've read the reports on the Senate hearings." His voice was soft but filled with fury. "I don't need you to tell me again."

Tanner leaned forward, bracing his arms on the bed as he smoothed back a strand of golden hair from Dawn's cheek. He was aware of Seth's eyes narrowing, the way he stiffened at Tanner's easy familiarity with the woman.

"She likes you," Tanner said softly. "Dawn doesn't like many men, you know."

Seth raised his gaze from Dawn's face once again, his expression dark, forbidding.

"What do you want, Tanner?" he asked, his patience obviously strained.

Tanner grinned at that. He strained everyone's patience. Everyone except Dawn's, that is.

"Don't let her go," he finally said softly. "When she wakes up, all the wounds that have healed since Dayan's death will be reopened. She'll withdraw and try to forget there's a life to be led other than fighting. Don't let her do it."

Seth's eyes narrowed.

Tanner could see why Dawn was attracted to him. He was a lot like Callan, quiet and sure, but strong enough to fight when he needed to. If any man could deal with the past she had suffered, it would be Seth.

"I hadn't intended to," he said with cool authority. "What makes you think I had?"

Tanner shook his head. "She's different. A lot of men don't like that. Dawn will kill a man faster than she'll consider kissing one. She's never been touched by a lover and if one tried it would likely terrify her. You don't have an easy fight on your hands."

"I won't fight her." Seth shook his head then. "I just won't leave. The rest will be Dawn's decision, Tanner. Not yours and not mine."

Tanner turned back to stare at his sister's silent face.

"Let's hope you're afforded that choice, my friend," Tanner said as he rose to his feet. "I'll be leaving soon. I won't be here to watch over her. And I want you to know, if you hurt her, I'll kill you myself."

Seth's gaze turning mocking. "Why don't you claim her yourself, Tanner?" he asked sarcastically.

Tanner smiled and shook his head. He had a feeling it was a good thing he didn't see Dawn in a sexual light, he wouldn't relish the thought of battling it out with the gutter fighter it was reported Seth Lawrence was.

"She's not mine to claim," he finally said. "If she was, I would have already and this conversation wouldn't be taking place. But never doubt I don't love her, Seth. I always will. And as sure as the bastard who touched her yesterday is a dead man, so will you be, if you hurt her. Remember that one."

He left the room before the other man could reply. Outside, Cabal leaned lazily against the wall, watching him curiously.

"Threats don't work with everyone, Tanner," he said coolly as he pushed back the black-streaked golden-brown hair from his face.

They were two parts of each other, he and Cabal. Not exactly brothers, but images of the same creature and often with opposing personalities. Where Tanner laughed, loved and enjoyed each day as it came, Cabal questioned and probed and gave little consideration to love.

"It was a promise," Tanner grunted. "Everything ready?"

"Packed and loaded." Cabal nodded as he straightened away from the wall. "You sure about this?"

Tanner smiled, baring his teeth in a savage grin of anticipation. "Oh yeah, I'm damned sure. Let's see what Council member Tallant thinks when it's his daughter he believes is being abused. Breed Law, Cabal, has many, many loopholes."

Also by Lora Leigh:

Also by Lora Leigh (continued):

About the author:

Lora Leigh is a 36-year-old wife and mother living in Kentucky. She dreams in bright, vivid images of the characters intent on taking over her writing life, and fights a constant battle to put them on the hard drive of her computer before they can disappear as fast as they appeared.

Lora's family, and her writing life co-exist, if not in harmony, in relative peace with each other. An understanding husband is the key to late nights with difficult scenes, and stubborn characters. His insights into human nature, and the workings of the male psyche provide her hours of laughter, and innumerable romantic ideas that she works tirelessly to put into effect.

Lora Leigh welcomes mail from readers. You can write to her c/o Ellora's Cave Publishing at 1056 Home Avenue, Akron OH 44310-3502.

Why an electronic book?

We live in the Information Age—an exciting time in the history of human civilization in which technology rules supreme and continues to progress in leaps and bounds every minute of every hour of every day. For a multitude of reasons, more and more avid literary fans are opting to purchase e-books instead of paperbacks. The question to those not yet initiated to the world of electronic reading is simply: *why?*

1. *Price.* An electronic title at Ellora's Cave Publishing and Cerridwen Press runs anywhere from 40-75% less than the cover price of the <u>exact same title</u> in paperback format. Why? Cold mathematics. It is less expensive to publish an e-book than it is to publish a paperback, so the savings are passed along to the consumer.

2. *Space.* Running out of room to house your paperback books? That is one worry you will never have with electronic novels. For a low one-time cost, you can purchase a handheld computer designed specifically for e-reading purposes. Many e-readers are larger than the average handheld, giving you plenty of screen room. Better yet, hundreds of titles can be stored within your new library—a single microchip. (Please note that Ellora's Cave and Cerridwen Press does not endorse any specific brands. You can check our website at www.ellorascave.com or

www.cerridwenpress.com for customer recommendations we make available to new consumers.)

3. *Mobility.* Because your new library now consists of only a microchip, your entire cache of books can be taken with you wherever you go.

4. *Personal preferences are accounted for.* Are the words you are currently reading too small? Too large? Too...**ANNOYING**? Paperback books cannot be modified according to personal preferences, but e-books can.

5. *Instant gratification.* Is it the middle of the night and all the bookstores are closed? Are you tired of waiting days—sometimes weeks—for online and offline bookstores to ship the novels you bought? Ellora's Cave Publishing sells instantaneous downloads 24 hours a day, 7 days a week, 365 days a year. Our e-book delivery system is 100% automated, meaning your order is filled as soon as you pay for it.

Those are a few of the top reasons why electronic novels are displacing paperbacks for many an avid reader. As always, Ellora's Cave and Cerridwen Press welcomes your questions and comments. We invite you to email us at service@ellorascave.com, service@cerridwenpress.com or write to us directly at: 1056 Home Ave. Akron OH 44310-3502.

Cerridwen, the Celtic Goddess of wisdom, was the muse who brought inspiration to storytellers and those in the creative arts. Cerridwen Press encompasses the best and most innovative stories in all genres of today's fiction. Visit our site and discover the newest titles by talented authors who still get inspired - much like the ancient storytellers did, once upon a time.

CERRIDWEN PRESS

www.cerridwenpress.com

THE
✟ ELLORA'S CAVE ✟
LIBRARY

Stay up to date with Ellora's Cave Titles in
Print with our Quarterly Catalog.

TO RECIEVE A CATALOG,
SEND AN EMAIL WITH YOUR NAME
AND MAILING ADDRESS TO:

CATALOG@ELLORASCAVE.COM

OR SEND A LETTER OR POSTCARD
WITH YOUR MAILING ADDRESS TO:

CATALOG REQUEST
C/O ELLORA'S CAVE PUBLISHING, INC.
1056 HOME AVENUE
AKRON, OHIO 44310-3502